SILVIE'S CHOICE

VIOLA TEMPEST

CONTENTS

Silvie's Choice

VIOLA TEMPEST

CHAPTER
ONE

AT THE DAWN OF TIME, ON TOP OF THE GREAT mountain called the Reach of Heaven, the palace, with the mountain as its floor and the sky as its roof, had gathered the gods in a great council hall. The fae deities arrived at the summit, and their leader, Kami, sat on the throne of clouds and looked out over her thirteen sisters. They stood around her in a semi-circle, dressed in flowing gowns made from the colors of the rainbow. Twinkling like the very stars themselves.

Also invited, was the horrible and grotesque Makung. Scaly and taloned, he crawled into the great council hall on all fours, casting glances in all directions. The fae gods were beautiful creatures, different, yet similar in their grace, with almond-shaped eyes, pointed ears, and a fair complexion.

The last god to join the council was the Lord of War and Destruction, Kurata. He strode in carrying his copper spear, dressed in a chestplate made from bronze, and had a red cape strewn around his back.

"Welcome, Lord Kurata," Kami said with disdain in her voice. "I am honored that you could join us, little brother."

"The honor is mine, sister." Kurata removed his helmet and released greasy strands of brown hair. "What is *that* doing here?"

Kurata pointed to Makung with the tip of his spear. The horrible creature shied away from it nervously.

"Lord Makung is one of us," Kaneda said and moved closer. "Makung is one of our siblings, as are you, Kurata."

"This is a council for all the deities in the universe," Kami added. "All are welcome."

"Then tell me of your agenda, sister," Kurata demanded sternly. "So that I might be on my way and not be offended by the smell of that creature or the sight of my sisters."

"Why do you think so little of us?" Kami asked, but then looked away.

"I have no love for such horrendous beings," Kurata replied. "You may not be as scaly and as rough as Makung here, with his yellow eyes and jagged teeth, but your slanted features and pointed ears are an affront to me."

"You believe yourself to be the perfect specimen, then?" Mitsue shot back with ferocity.

"I do, dear sister," spat Kurata. "Look at my height, my masculine physique, my strength. My strong, sharp features and hairy body. It's what one aspires to."

"Maybe to you, brother," Kami replied, "but I do not believe all would think so."

"Then a friendly competition on the matter, then?" Kurata smiled, and his eyes narrowed.

"A competition?" Kaneda asked. "In that how one measures beauty? And who would judge such a competition?"

"We create our judges!" Kurata threw out his arms.

"Now I know you are addled." Khan laughed.

"Do not laugh at me, sister, lest you find yourself impaled by this blade." Kurata reached for the sword at his side.

"Please be calm." Kami raised a hand. "It might not be such a bad idea."

"Explain, Kami." Khan turned to her.

"I have heard rumors of other gods in other parts of this universe who have created beings in their image." Kami looked over to the west.

"How do you mean?" Kaneda inquired. "We have populated this world with wild beasts. Do you mean we create another creature?"

"Close." Kami held up a finger. "We create them from our image, to resemble us. All of them with our abilities, strengths, and weaknesses. Whichever creature survives throughout the ages is the best, and therefore, a symbol of their creator's greatness."

"I like this." Kurata scratched his beard. "My creation would be strong, competitive, and tenacious. Sure to win. At least, over whatever Makung could make."

"You feel very self-assured." Makung moved closer to his little brother. "There are abilities in this body that you will never possess or command."

"Get away from me!" Kurata looked down in disgust. "Your beings and my miraculous creations will be mortal enemies. The jealousy your vile things would feel toward my wondrous beings will cast them into darkness forever."

"You make a bold prediction, Kurata." Makung

slithered back toward one of the giant pillars holding up the sky. "You better be ready to wipe up the pieces of your creations from the universe."

"Let us all calm down," Kami said and held up her hand again. "We are in agreement, then? Each of us, the faes, Kurata, and Makung, create a creature in our image to inhabit the worlds down below. Whichever creature survives through the ages will represent the winner."

"I agree." Kurata nodded his head.

"As do I," Makung whispered.

Kami looked over to her sisters. They all nodded in unison also.

Suddenly, the air changed. A great sorrow fell over the Reach of Heaven, and the sky darkened as the sound of large wings thundered across the mountain range. The gods looked up at the sky as a large body came toward them from above.

All of them, except for Kurata, moved back as a large reptilian creature landed on four legs among them. A pair of leathery wings reached out to either side, threatening to topple the pillars next to it.

It was red, with a long and scaly body, like that of a serpent. The legs ended in four clawed feet that scratched at the ground, leaving deep gashes in the stone. The head resembled that of an ancient lizard, and sharp teeth glistened in the sunlight, while a forked tongue lolled out of the gigantic maw. The dragon, for a dragon he was, turned his horned head and observed the stoic gods.

"I heard rumors of a great council meeting among the clouds," he growled. "A council meeting where all the gods were invited. In the sky. Yet I, the Dragon Lord, god of the sky, was not extended with an invitation."

"You are no deity," Kami said and rose from her seat. "You were spawned from the unholy fires deep inside the very rock on which we stand."

"I *am* a god," the Dragon Lord roared and spit fire into the air. The Reach council shook in terror. "Who are you to deny me the right to stand amongst you?"

"I am Kami. Leader of the gods, the eldest daughter of Time and Space. That is my claim to godhood. What pray tell is yours?"

The Dragon Lord crawled toward Kami and came to stand eye to eye with her, his hot breath singeing her dress.

"What is my claim?" he snarled. "Do you want me to tell you?"

"Get away from her!" Kurata screamed and stood between his sister and the dragon.

"Kurata." Kami put a hand on her brother's shoulder. "I can handle this."

"Stay back, sister." Kurata looked over his shoulder.

"I shall deal with this beast. I thought it was bad enough that my parents had bore such a hideous creature as Makung into this universe, but this excrement that has exuded from the rocks is more of an abomination than I can tolerate."

"Do as you wish, god." The Dragon Lord moved back at the sight of Kurata's hand on the hilt of his blade. "I am merely here to be accepted by this council. Any decision made here, I should be a part of."

"On what grounds?" Kaneda stepped in.

"On the grounds that the sky is mine." The Dragon Lord hovered his head in rage and snarled again. "It is my domain."

"You have no domain," Kami protested behind the back of Kurata. "We do not wish for your attendance or for your input. In fact, we cast you out!"

"You shall do no such thing." The Dragon Lord came at her with his sharp, fierce claws and maw.

Kurata unsheathed his blade and sliced the great dragon across the chest, shaving off the protective layer of scales. The action made the dragon scream, and he looked down. His belly and chest were exposed. Soft, tender flesh clearly visible.

"One more swing of my blade, and your insides will wet the floor of this hallowed place." Kurata stood ready for the next pounce, a fiery hot rage piercing through his eyes.

The Dragon Lord sunk back, fully aware that he had been bested.

"So be it, gods." He spat and spewed smoke from his nostrils. "Have your little council meeting and realm. But know this, I will forever be here to disrupt your world, at every corner."

And with one great leap, he jumped into the sky and flew away, soaring high in between the clouds.

"I owe you my life, brother," Kami said as Kurata turned around.

"I know you could have held your own," he smiled, "but I was itching for a fight. Naturally, this changes nothing pertaining to our contest."

"Of course not." Kami agreed and nodded her head.

Each of the deities retreated back to their homes, so they could craft a unique creature in their own image to inhabit each of the worlds, all with different perspectives of what the mightiest of the mighty should look like.

Makung created the hideous onis, scaly and horrid, with giant claws and garbled speech. Kaneda created the dryads, and Khan, the naiads, while the other fae gods created the other faes, such as the pixies, gnomes, elves, and so forth. Kurata created the humans, hungry for power, domination, and war.

Kami, the last of them, created the kitsunes, and

she imbued them with her beauty, power, and, best of all, strength. She looked at them in awe as they took their first steps, a mix of hers and Kurata's best traits, an homage to her brother for saving her life.

In the dark of a faraway mountain, the Dragon Lord had learned the secret of creating life. He made the dragons in his own image, and even fashioned them a home. They would forever be the thorn in the side of the Reach council... and all their creatures of abomination.

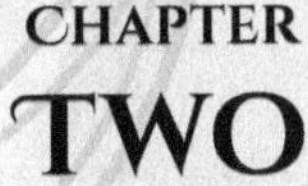

CHAPTER
TWO

It was a cold, gray morning. The sun was only a hint through the misty clouds that had enveloped the mountains ranging in the distance. Silvie stood prepared on the parapet, her pet kitsune companion and friend beside her, and her hand on the hilt of her curved blade. She tapped it while she raised her left arm to shield her eyes from what little light permeated through the fog. She could hear the distant rumbling of crude war drums at the foot of the range.

The familiar and ominous rhythm of the beating had always signaled the coming of danger and trouble. The creatures that fashioned them had little artisanal skill, making use of whatever they could acquire from various battlefields. For they were scavengers.

"They have breached the range," Tekasun said as he placed a hand on her shoulder.

She turned to look at him. He was already dressed in his bamboo chest armor and black kimono, the items symbolizing that he was prepared for battle.

"Is it just me," Silvie began, "or do the creatures traverse the mountains with more ease over these past few years?"

"According to the elders, they've evolved," Tekasun replied. "When a swarm of them attempts to scale the mountains and fail, they breed stronger beasts, and then try again. How they do it is a curiosity in which I cannot understand."

It was true.

For centuries, the kitsunes, one of the last original thirteen fae tribes in the Far East, had made their home in the Golden Valley. A fertile area surrounded by vast and treacherous mountains, pushed north by various invading tribes. The natural walls of ice and snow had become their protection from the invading outsiders, but as time passed, and the kitsunes became more legend and lore than historical fact as others came looking for them.

After centuries of living in harmony, the faes had begun to grate against each other. They were prolific, and soon, any land to inhabit became sparse. This would become the kindling on which a great fire would ignite and spread.

It started simply enough with the lack of food. Most of the various faes were avid hunters or gatherers, not farmers like the children of Kurata, the humans. And this caused a problem when more faes spread out, and the abundance of food dwindled further.

This would be the beginning of the first fae war, of which there would be three. It quickly diminished the population, and as the wildlife, berries, and fruits returned, most of the thirteen creatures made in the fae deities' images were gone.

Eons earlier, the kitsune elders made the decision to flee to the Golden Valley, the famed birthplace of their race. According to the legend, Kami had fashioned the first male and female kitsune from the fertile soil of the valley, then dribbled water from the stream that flowed from the mountains onto them. Cool and crisp, it came from the ice and snow that melted beneath the morning sun. It had given the kitsunes their distinctive golden complexion and cool demeanor.

Once the kitsunes made their exodus from the rest of the world and settled in the valley, they began to construct their golden city. They kept the name "Golden Valley" as they saw it as the perfect name for their new haven. With an abundance of natural resources, and bestowed with the creativity and ingenuity of their creator, they had built something truly magnificent.

The influx of humans had pushed the other creatures to the outer rims of the known universe. The children of Kurata's own ingenuity rivaled that of the wisest kitsunes, but instead of using it for creativity and splendor, the humans fashioned weapons and armor. Used their wise men and women to devise plans to eradicate the other races.

They had also grown in numbers, and they needed space to live in, all at the cost of the faes and onis alike. Forcing them to the sea in the east, the desert in the south, the deep woods in the west, and the mountains in the north. This caused these creatures to attempt a massive invasion of the valley in search for refuge of their own.

Silvie found humans, though she had never encountered one, to be a nuisance. Her father had told her of how they'd changed the fae world and done irrevocable harm to it. While the faes and onis had been created to live and settle in the universe, the humans were forced to adapt.

Kurata had not created them to become evolved at inception. No, he had perhaps given them the greatest gift of all, the ability to adapt to their surroundings. Blessed them with an innate will to conquer their surroundings, and this meant that they had to learn and face challenges, but also deal with the curse of not being able to calculate consequences. This made them more powerful and dangerous than any of the other creations. Without any concern for their own well-being or that of any other race, they exploded onto the universe, interrupting and destroying anything that might come in their way.

This led to a great deal of conflict amongst them-selves, something the faes and onis never experienced. In the end, the humans *did* have some sense of self-preservation, and thus, settled down, not only in order to survive, but they came to the realization that war did not put food on the table, especially if the world they were to steal from had died out.

A fragile sense of peace eventually spread across the land, however, very temporarily.

And if the humans wreaked havoc onto the world they shared with the other races, the dragons were even worse.

Once all powerful beings, they had become nothing more than a mere legend. They had been struck the worst by the advent of men, forced to hide their serpentine bodies underground. It'd been decades since anyone had seen one of them as they hid in the shadows.

The Dragon Lord chose to gift them with more rage and nothing else, and they lacked the skills to cooperate with each other, rendering them solitary creatures that attacked the other races at their own free will.

Human figures called "heroes" set out to eradicate these beasts with great success, and eventually, they vanished, making scholars suspect that they had simply died out, or maybe never existed at all.

In the known universe, no proof of them remained. No bones, no eggs, no memories.

CHAPTER

THREE

"WHAT'S THE GOOD NEWS?" AN ARMORED WOMAN asked as she scaled the parapet. Her long black hair was hidden under a glistening helmet, with feathers attached to the top.

"The enemies are approaching, Silvie," Tekasun replied. "Just like the scouts had indicated."

"What is it this time?" Sungi asked as she walked up to them.

"Hard to tell," Silvie replied. "Could be anything at this point."

"It feels like we've just beaten off a horde of kappas," Sungi chimed and plucked a spyglass from her belt.

"That was a fortnight ago." Tekasun smiled. "You've got to keep up, Sungi."

The kappas were wild beasts forged from the unholy alliance of onis and dryads. No fae would willingly give themselves to an oni, but during the Second Fae War, a tribe of onis raided an already ravaged dryad village, pillaging all their resources and forcing the unsuspecting and vulnerable dryads to mate with them.

The result was the horrendous hybrid race known as the kappa. Half oni, half dryad. The sheer idea of it was enough to give any kitsune nightmares. They had the scaly, hairless body of the onis, but walked upright like the dryads.

Silvie shuddered at the memory of the hideous creatures that attempted to penetrate the valley. Most of the time, she would be over the mountain range fighting off raiders, but these things had closed in on the very walls of their home.

"At this rate, we'll be fighting enemies every week, if not every day," she said with a sigh.

When she was training to become a kitsune warrior, and a part of the Order of the Fox, she had never imagined that she'd be fighting this often.

Her father had put her in training at the young age of six, and from that day on, she'd been training every day. A rigorous and seemingly never-ending routine of physical and mental drills, as well as weapons management and strategy. The Order of the Fox were a group of legendary fighters and were feared throughout the land of the faes. Honing their skills throughout the fae wars.

According to the legend, the kitsune elder, Kaya, who was excellent in his own right, had formed the order when he realized that an impending war was approaching. He trained a few kitsune warriors to become what he envisioned to be the strongest fighters in the known universe. To become one with their surroundings, their blades extensions of their arms. Crafty and cunning like the animal form from whom they took their name.

At the beginning, they wore only black tunics made from the finest silk, for Kaya believed that if the kitsunes could not avoid being hit, then they deserved to be injured. This would be rectified after the first several skirmishes, as the warriors soon realized that it was unavoidable to be struck during a hail of arrows raining down upon them. They took whatever they had at hand, and wanting to forgo the awkwardness of a metal breastplate, they opted for the more pliable, yet durable, bamboo. They still wore the silken kimonos for maximum movement, however.

Soon, other kitsune villages and towns followed suit. They brought in elite members of the order to train a new batch of warriors, and they took the name of other animals, like tigers, bears, and hawks. Each of them with their own unique fighting style.

Soon, the kitsunes became known as the "warrior fae." The name fit them well, with their tall, lanky frame, and were deceptively strong as they dressed in billowy fabrics that hid their muscles. Each of the warrior tribes chose their own weapon as well, and the Foxes bore their traditional curved blade, known to some as a scimitar. Kaya had seen the weapon during his travels to the west and decided to quickly adapt it as his.

All this gave the kitsunes an edge against the other faes, allowing them to win battle after battle and making them feared throughout the Far East.

Some of warriors, like Silvie's brother, Aoki, became soldiers of fortune, leaving the shelter of the valley behind to fight for someone else's cause. They formed their own enclaves among others, minor kitsune clans that had either survived or decided to stay on the outside. This was looked down on by the elders, who found no honor in it, but the other kitsunes, like Aoki, were tired of remaining sheltered and wished to experience the rest of the world.

"What are you doing?" Silvie had asked him while he packed his bag with the few items that he owned.

The Order of the Foxes kept a vow of poverty. Limiting the amount of possessions they had. Two changes of clothes, boots, and so forth. The less they owned, the better it was.

"I need to get out of this place," Aoki said and looked at her with his almond-shaped eyes.

They were blue, quite different from her olive green ones. But apart from that, it was quite obvious that they were siblings. The same slender faces with sharp angular chins and sunken cheeks, and pale complexions like the rest of their people. Kitsunes were not as stunningly beautiful as the dryads or the naiads, the aquatic faes on the western border, but beautiful enough to turn heads when surrounded by others.

"What's wrong with the valley?" Silvie asked and placed a hand on his bag to halt him, forcing him to look at her. "It's our home. Where we grew up, and where our parents grew up before us."

"You don't think I know that?" Aoki asked rhetorically and turned away.

He stared out the small window that looked over the village. It was dark outside; the light from the homes scattered throughout looked like the stars in a night sky.

"So, then why leave?" Silvie came up behind him once again.

"There is nothing here for me anymore," he replied and shied away from her. "I'm tired of fighting these endless battles."

"Are you saying you want to quit the order?" Silvie felt stunned at this turn of events.

"No, not at all." Aoki turned toward her, head bowed. "I'm just tired of always being on the defensive side. There is something within me yearning for more. I'm not ready to settle down with a female yet and have children, only to scale those walls and cut down attackers when time called for it."

"Then what do you want?" she questioned him, her tone more tense. "What do you yearn for, Aoki?"

"I want to be out there, fighting my own battles." He returned the same tension as he replied. "I want to be the aggressor, the offense. The one who takes his destiny in his own hands. I'm tired of always being on the defense, waiting, and waiting, and waiting. I want it all to be on my terms."

Silvie fell silent. She had nothing left to say. No comment or remark to throw back in return. Aoki came up to her and placed his hand on her shoulder, trying to comfort her.

"I need to feel the freedom that's outside of this valley," he whispered. "I need to experience what the world beyond our village has to offer. I might end up in another kitsune village, meet some other faes, and live with them, or climb aboard a ship bound for foreign shores. Who knows where my journey shall take me?"

"I understand." Silvie placed her hand on his and patted it. "I know what you're saying, but ever since the deaths of mother and father, you're all I have left." She looked away. "It's selfish, I know that, but I can't help it."

"Then come with me, Silvie." Aoki grabbed her chin with his finger and thumb, lifting her head up. "Why stay here and stagnate?"

"I can't leave," she mumbled. She tried to fight back her tears, knowing fully well that what she was about to say next would separate them from each other forever. "I am bound by my duty and honor to stay here. The world out there frightens me. I know that's such a silly thing to say, especially coming from a member of the order, but it's the truth. I don't have any interest or curiosity in finding out what's on the other side of the mountains. I want to defend the one home I have, not wander aimlessly for a new one."

That was it. The last word in their conversation.

The following morning, she watched her brother, bag over one shoulder, wander away from the Golden Valley. Toward the mountains and the outside world.

SILVIE EVENTUALLY HEARD THAT HE HAD FOUND another kitsune tribe way down south and joined them, settled in, and built a family, but they were all just mere rumors and speculation. He didn't send her a letter, telling her that he was okay, not even an oral message with any of the kitsune travelers who came to call on them.

She asked them all about him, but they only claimed that they might have seen a kitsune fitting Aoki's description in some village or town. It hurt. It hurt her to the core, but as time passed, so did the pain, and eventually, she started to forget some of her memories about him. His smell, the way he looked at her, and the touch of his warm hands. The way he would sneak up behind her and wrap his arms around her frame. Kissing her gently on the head.

"I'm here," he would whisper. "Everything's going to be okay."

CHAPTER

FOUR

"Oni," Sungi said as she lowered the instrument.

"Oni?" Tekasun asked.

"Yes, a horde of onis are quickly coming down the hill," she replied. "They seem bigger than the last ones we saw. Arms bigger, claws sharper, all equipped to scale the city walls."

"Damn it," Silvie whispered under her breath. "We need to sound the alarm, then. This is more than just firing arrows from high above like last time."

"Indeed, it is," Tekasun replied and headed over to the large brass bell at the end of the walkway.

The elders had forged the ancient artifact from various metals found within the mountains, or so the story was told, and was designed to warn the kitsunes of impending enemy attacks. According to the legend of the kitsune elders, they'd created it when they first settled in the valley. The memories of gruesome battles and fatal casualties had forced them to create a warning signal to mobilize the warriors quicker, and it worked!

The scouts up in the towers that surrounded the village would send a flaming arrow into the air, signaling imminent danger. And the watchers, old widows with nothing but time on their hands, would then immediately ring the bell, four times to be exact, to awaken the rest of the village.

When the enemies were easily dealt with, the Foxes never bothered sounding it. The guards had learned which ones they were over the years, and in those instances, they would dispatch them quickly and quietly. But at times when a battle was difficult to hide from others, and the prospect of creatures actually coming into the city proper was high, then the bell must toll.

Silvie looked over at Tekasun as he purposefully strode toward the end of the parapet and looked up at the tower that housed the ancient object. They could see it hanging from the vast ceiling, looking at it as the bell slowly swayed back and forth in the slight breeze of the autumn morning.

Seasons came and went in the Golden Valley, but not like in the rest of the world. Even though it laid in the very far north, the vast mountain range functioned as a protective ring around the valley, creating a temperate zone where the seasons blended into one another. This made the winter mild with a steady rain as opposed to snow, gave autumn and spring a sense of warmth and ever-changing colors, and the summer was often presented with a slight breeze coming off the snow-capped mountains.

Silvie turned her gaze toward the city as it slowly awoken from its slumber. She could see, hear, and smell all the hustle and bustle in the market square that was located at the foot of the Great Temple with its golden spires.

From the square, various artisans like bakers, butchers, and blacksmiths were all sprawled out. The sound of the blacksmith hammering away on iron echoed up toward her as it intermingled with the smell of the freshly baked bread, which also blended with the shouts and laughter of the fruit and vegetable merchants.

It was the symphony of her home, and in that moment, she remembered why she had stayed behind, why she hadn't gone with Aoki that fateful night when he walked out of her life. Possibly forever. That was why she remained on the parapet and defended it with every fiber of her being. She did it for the beautiful structures. She did it for the kitsunes who dwelled in them. She did it for her god.

The temple acted as a hub for the village, with blocks of homes spreading out like the spokes of a wheel in all directions. Old stone homes of the richer families toward the middle, with old rickety homes spread along the city walls... the first to go if there were ever a breach.

It was meant to look like a wheel, and the wheel symbolized life. It was the ancient mark of Kami, the one she had placed next to the first kitsune. At the altar of the temple, a gilded wheel, intricately carved, hung. Visitors would kneel before it as they prayed to their god for protection, help, or simply just to offer their gratitude.

Some claimed that it was the same wheel that Kami had left them, imbued with commandments on how the kitsunes should live. Those words were etched into the golden spokes, but not one kitsune, not even the priests who lived and worked in the temple, could read the ancient tongue. So, they interpreted them.

Silvie had always found this suspicious, as there were times when she was certain that the commandments changed. She didn't bother with them, though, and in the end, neither did any of the other kitsunes. They never seemed to change to any particular kitsune's agenda, so why argue?

The temple, along with the palace, made up the hub of the city. While the temple stood tall over the other buildings, large and ostentatious in honor of Kami, the palace was a low building made from black lacquered wooden frames and white paper walls. These walls were decorated with images of past rulers and important elders. The kitsunes were not ruled by any king per se, but instead, by the head of the council of elders. But still, they used the title of "king," for they had no better name to use.

The position was passed to the oldest member of the council, and then remained with that kitsune until death came to take them away. The palace functioned more as a meeting place for the elders, where they discussed the crucial topics of the day. Once these discussions were well and truly done, the king would rule on it and make a final decision. Among the elders, sat the High Priest and the General of the Foxes. The idea had always been that there should be representatives from all facets of the kitsune society.

Every time Silvie stood watch over the Golden Valley, be it night or day, she felt in awe of the magnificent city, with its many homes, towers, and gilded roofs. The kitsunes had built something awe-inspiring within the mountains. A self-contained, sprawling, and wondrous place to live, sheltered from most others in the Far East. They used the resources at hand, gold from the river flowing through, iron from the rolling hills, and fruits and vegetables from the fertile soil.

No wonder the others in the fae kingdom also wished to settle here. No wonder the hordes of faes or onis crashed toward the city walls like waves against a dam.

The bell rang with a heavy sound. It echoed down the valley and through the cobbled streets as kitsunes awoken from it. Tekasun struck it again, and then a third time. Silvie watched as the other kitsunes looked up at the tower, stepping out of their homes or places of business to discuss this latest alarm with one another. They had gotten used to the bell ringing a couple of times a month, and had long since ceased their waves of panic whenever the alarm sounded.

It was both good and bad. Even though they knew that danger was on its way, they had become desensitized by the constant threats. But in addition to that, they weren't afraid. They had complete trust in the council and relied on them to protect their safety. Just like they had whenever an attacker came their way.

"What is it this time?" General Naito asked as he rose from his early morning slumber to scale the wall.

The general elder had the weathered look that every kitsune got as they aged. A kitsune could live well into their thousands. Like the other faes, they had been gifted with longevity and an immunity to illness, which in a way, made them superior to the humans, who fell ill all the time.

General Naito wore a thin gray mustache under his bony nose. Only the oldest of the kitsunes could grow facial hair, and once they did, they wore it like a badge. His skin had turned from light and pale to a leathery complexion that had been weathered by the elements. He wore a black kimono, but with a silvery embroidered trim. His bamboo chestplate had also been painted silver in order for him to stand out on the battlefield.

Silvie had been told that it was a way to draw attention from the enemy, so that the foot soldiers could move behind enemy lines.

General Naito's chestplate didn't quite fit him, though. He had gained a considerable amount of weight over the past years, something that was usually common among older kitsunes. It signaled that he was close to his final years in this universe.

The kitsunes believed that when they passed onto the next world, they became one with the soil that once birthed them, as Kami first breathed life into the first kitsune. Most of the other faes also believed the same. The naiads believed that they went back to the life-giving streams from which they were formed, and the dryads back to the trees from whose bark they were fashioned.

One day, if he didn't die in battle first, General Naito would walk outside the Great Wall and lie down on the grass. Allow the flowers to cover him, and then close his eyes in order to breathe his last breath and silently pass away.

Kitsunes always knew when it was time to go; they felt it in their bones. They would say their goodbyes the day before, accepting their final fate. Some would even host elaborate feasts, but most of them would simply have a contemplative family dinner with their loved ones, and then leave the following morning.

Their family would watch them leave from atop the wall, and then watch them as they lied down to rest. That evening, as the sun set, they would head outside and build a pyre, where they would place the lifeless body. It was beautiful in its own way.

"We are looking at a horde of onis coming down

the hill," Silvie said as the large fae hurled himself over the parapet.

"Why sound the alarm?" Naito spat with anger. "We've vanquished an entire horde just a month ago."

"We did," Tekasun replied. "But these seem more equipped to scale our walls. They also seem bigger and scalier. I think they might pose a real threat."

Naito grabbed the spyglass from Sungi and shot a glance over the distance. They waited a while as the general scanned the horizon carefully. He allowed the spyglass to move back and forth a few times before quickly removing it from his eye.

"By the gods," the general exclaimed. "Man the walls with every warrior we have available. Let's make short work of these things."

"Everything seem normal?" Silvie asked as she, Tekasun, and Sungi followed the general across the wall.

"I would say not." Naito stared purposefully ahead as he strode across the parapet. "Those onis don't look like anything we've ever seen before. Their coloring seems different, and as you said, Tekasun, their scales are different, as are their arms and legs. I think we are seeing a new breed here."

"Like how the kappas were a new breed?" Sungi asked.

"Maybe." Naito stopped and looked at them. "But

there is nothing in those hideous creatures that hint at onis or faes, or even humans."

"What are they, then?" Sungi asked.

"Something completely new, perhaps." Naito scratched his chin. "Whatever they are, we shall prevail. Assemble the warriors, now! Let's not get caught up in the unknown."

Moments later, two rows of two hundred kitsune warriors lined up alongside Silvie, Tekasun, and Sungi, hands tightly gripping their curved blades or bows. Most of them had been in this situation before, patiently waiting for the enemy to approach. They were stoic, not moving a muscle, just allowing the breeze to caress their pale faces.

Then they emerged from the mist at the foot of the wall. Hundreds of creatures. Their muscular and naked bodies tinted a bluish green. Snarling maws howling with the thirst for blood. Horns protruded from their giant heads, with large yellow eyes darting in all directions. They crawled on all fours, with small wing-like appendages protruding from their backs.

They didn't pause to take in the massive wall before them. Instead, they proceeded to scale it, sinking their claws into the stone masonry with ease. Some fluttered the appendages that seemed to act as wings and rose up into the sky, but just a few feet, so that they could more easily grab the cracks that were in between the bricks.

"Fire!" Naito cried.

The archers fired a volley of arrows down at the bluish green beasts. Their sinewy bodies were so hard and scaly that most of the projectiles simply bounced off. But the arrows that did manage to land on the creatures, piercing their eyes, necks, and mouths, caused the creatures to cry out in pain and tumble to the ground.

As the sun continued to rise behind the curtain of mist, the onis came over the wall. They were met by the fierce kitsune warriors who cut them down with ease. The sharp blades sliced through the tough skin, severing limbs and creating gaping wounds.

Silvie breathed heavily as wave after wave of beasts came at her. She closed her eyes and remembered her training. Simply allowing the blade to swing from side to side, slicing and cutting in a beautiful pattern. She felt the edge dig into the scales, scraping them without the familiar sinking into flesh. It felt like she was shaving over a rock, but she continued the movement, convinced that it would pierce something soon enough.

Suddenly, the attack stopped, and everything fell silent. Silvie opened her eyes again to see the beasts standing still, not moving an inch.

"What's happening?" she whispered.

Tekasun shrugged.

Sungi took a step forward and feigned an attack at one of the creatures, and it didn't even flinch. Instead, it looked up into the sky, staring at the low clouds hanging over them like a large fluffy blanket. She did the same, lowering her blade as the rest of the battle-field fell silent. Not a single body moved in the tranquil autumn morning. And the sun was the only thing piercing the morning mist.

Then they heard it. The unmistakable flapping of large leathery wings. The air suffocated with tension. The sound multiplied, surrounding them at all sides.

"This can't be," Naito whispered loudly with a trembling voice as he gripped the hilt of his curved blade tightly.

Then out of the mist, they emerged.

The long, red serpentine bodies of dragons.

THE FIRE GENTLY CRACKLED IN THE OPEN HEARTH at the center of the square tall building. The watchtower was built from extra hardened bamboo that could withstand the harsh climate of the South Sea. At times, the waves that crashed against the cliffs could rise up to eleven feet, deadly to any wayward fisherman caught unaware.

As the night fell, the storm came, and the howling wind of the autumn season beat against the tall structure. The violence of nature threatened to break the handcrafted tower, and if he hadn't known better, Aoki might have feared for his life. But after so many years in the south, he had grown accustomed to it. He placed another log onto the crackling fire and yawned.

"Late nights getting to you?" Asari laughed at him as he stepped out of the shadow.

"This is my third all-night shift," Aoki replied and looked up at the six-foot kitsune.

"By the spirits, this will be the death of us," Asari said and sat down on the log opposite him. He removed his straw hat, allowing the rain water to spill down onto the dirt floor.

"This, or the dragons," Aoki replied and threw a piece of bamboo from his chestplate into the blaze.

It had been close to a month since the dragons formed a unified attack on various kitsune strongholds and villages. It had thrown the worlds into unmitigated chaos. The humans, who had never seen a dragon before, were caught completely unaware and had scattered. Now, faes and humans alike were sitting in their watchtowers, or behind their walls, waiting for the next attack.

In truth, no one had seen a real dragon in years. Only the oldest of the faes might have come in contact with one when they were younger, but here they were again. Back for blood.

Everyone did a double duty shift in Preserve, the warriors known in this region as the Eagles. Aoki had wondered out loud if the late nights and lack of sleep would be detrimental to them once the dragons finally *did* decide to eradicate them.

Preserve was often seen as the last stronghold of the kitsunes outside the Golden Valley. It was placed on the banks of the South Sea, overlooking the treacherous water. It was a trading hub for both the humans and the faes. The only place in the Far East where the various races could meet in peace.

Trade was important. The abilities that the fae gods had bestowed upon their creations all made for various skills, each unique, and they had come to the conclusion that, should they survive in this harsh universe, they needed to trade with each other.

Preserve was also a harbor city. Ships went in and out of the docks that stretched over the sea, creating an inlet. Ships carrying goods from far away lands across the South Sea came in and out of the port. It was the only time the kitsunes ever came in contact with creatures other than the faes, humans, or onis. The creatures of the south were similar in appearance as them, but with different abilities, taller, and more muscular.

What god had spawned them, they did not know.

Suddenly, a heavy knock fell upon the door of the tower, the door made of tightly bundled bamboo reeds. Asari and Aoki looked at each other, perplexed. Who could possibly want to venture out into the storm that was raging outside? The kitsunes were burrowers, and a network of labyrinthine tunnels ran from the towers to the village proper, so there would be no need to use the outside door... for anyone who belonged there, at least. This could only mean one thing. An outsider.

"Why don't I get the door?" Asari offered. "You come behind me with your blade, ready to strike."

Aoki nodded. Asari outranked him by quite a bit, so the kitsune would be honor bound to investigate any strange occurrences, no matter how foolish it may seem.

"I don't think a dragon would knock," Aoki suggested with a slight chuckle.

"You never know," Asari replied. "They *are* crafty creatures, after all. Or so, they would have you believe."

Aoki smiled, then carefully rose from his seat, sliding his razor-sharp blade from its scabbard. He glided across the floor, watching the shadows from the hearth dance across the still shape of Asari, who held a steady hand on the doorknob. He held a rave-billed axe behind his back, the fiercest piece of weaponry the kitsunes knew of.

A thunderclap echoed overhead, and the night lit up in a white blinding light as the door swung open.

Asari stepped in front of the opening, the axe still hidden behind him. Standing in the pouring rain, battered by the intense wind, was a female kitsune. Her black hair danced in the wind while she desperately gripped what remained of her kimono. Her pale skin was almost translucent as it reflected the lightning against the dark sky.

"I am looking for Aoki," she said stoically.

Asari could see that she was trying to fight off the impact from the elements, that her warrior's code forbade her from showing how she shivered. He stepped off to the side to allow Aoki to see the kitsune fighting the elements on their doorstep.

"Silvie?" Aoki exclaimed and slid his blade back into its lacquered sheath. "What are you doing here?" He rushed over to her and grabbed her arm, pulling her indoors, safe from the elements. "I feared that you were dead," Aoki continued as he ushered Silvie to one of the seats by the hearth.

"I came close to being dead," Silvie replied and slid out of the wet clothes. "I could say the same for you, in all honesty." She winked at him and tried to smile.

Asari brought out a towel from their storage closet to keep her from being naked for a long period of time. Even so, he couldn't help but steal a glance of the beautiful creature standing in the warm glow of the crackling fire. He could see that her body was riddled with bruises and scorch marks, the brands of a recent battle.

She was also thin and looked emaciated. Time on the road must have been the reason. The journey from the Golden Valley to the South Sea was not a journey done quickly and painlessly. To start, it would have taken her several days to traverse the mountains, and then an additional month, at least, to travel across the land to this watchtower. That was, if she knew where to go.

"Thank you." She smiled at him.

"Pardon my manners," Aoki said as he walked over to her. "This is Tam Asari, second in command at Preserve."

"Pleasure to make your acquaintance." Silvie dried her hair without taking into consideration that she had completely disrobed. "When did you hear of the attack on the valley?" Silvie asked her brother.

"What do you mean?" Aoki asked in return.

"You said you thought I was dead. This could only be if you had known that we were attacked by the dragons." Silvie then wrapped the towel around her body.

Kitsune warriors were trained to see each other as bodies, not as males or females, as that would be a distraction on the field of battle, but in Preserve, there were such few female kitsunes among the Eagles that it became difficult not to.

"We got word of the attack close to a fortnight ago," Aoki said and raised an eyebrow at his sister. "Traders from up north brought us the news, but they told us that there were no survivors."

"None that they knew of," Asari added.

"Do you happen to have a spare kimono?" Silvie asked once she noticed Asari staring at her.

"Of course," Asari said, tearing his eyes off of her.

"What has brought you here, Silvie?" Aoki asked and handed his sister a terracotta mug of steaming hot broth that had been cooking on the hearth.

"I'm sure you've heard that those who attacked us were dragons," Silvie began.

"Same with most of the villages and towns," Aoki

added. "By the time the news reached us, the dragons had already attacked several of the villages north of here."

"True." She sipped the broth loudly. "We appear to have been the first ones in the attack. They targeted our best warriors." Silvie spoke softly as she stared into the fire. "I watched my friends, fellow Foxes, die. Consumed by the flames from the maws of those hideous beasts."

"They are not like us," Asari said when he returned and handed her a black kimono, emblazoned with a flying eagle on the chest. "They are pure evil, and they will stop at nothing to destroy our entire world."

"If you had told me that just a year ago, I wouldn't have believed you." Silvie grabbed the kimono and slipped it over her head. "But after having witnessed the attack first-hand, I know this to be true."

"Why do they want to attack the kitsunes?" Aoki asked.

"I think it's more than just our race," Asari replied. "Reports are coming in from all around of attacks on the other faes, and even on the humans."

"But no word on the reasoning behind it?" Silvie asked.

"According to our elders here in Preserve," Asari explained, "the dragons were bred from hate. Their creator made them to bring about chaos to our land. To kill every other race in the Far East. For what reason, well, that has been lost in time."

"So, some legendary feud is what fuels these creatures?" Aoki cringed at the thought of it.

"Who knows?" Asari answered. "The dragons don't seem to have a true leader, so negotiating with them is out of the question."

"All we can do is sit and wait for them to come here, and then deal with it." Aoki shrugged.

"They *will* come here." Silvie looked over at her brother. "You can count on that, but we don't have to die here. We can fight them, and we can win."

Aoki found a cot for his sister to sleep on. He guided her into the deepest section of the tower, past the sleeping quarters of the Eagle warriors, who were all sleeping soundly. The room he found for her was a little more than a pantry next to the armory, but Silvie was tired, and she didn't care. She only wanted somewhere to place her head and feel warm for the first time in over a month.

"How did you find me?" Aoki asked her as she sat down on the cot.

"Were you hoping I didn't?" Silvie patted the linens.

"I think you're being unfair." Aoki leaned against the doorframe.

"Really?" Silvie replied and squinted at him. "You were the one who left without sending word as to where you were."

"You knew that would happen." Aoki crossed his arms. "How many young men leave the valley, only to never be heard from again?"

"I know," Silvie replied. "But I didn't think my own brother would do the same. I thought our bond was stronger than that."

"What did you want me to do?" Aoki raised his voice.

"I wanted you to send word to me through messages to our home, to let me know where you were." Silvie was feeling frustrated at the conversation. "I wandered from the north to this place, stopping at villages and towns of both kitsunes, humans, naiads, and dryads, and no one knows where you are. Injured from the attack of dragons, scalded, then cold. Tired and beaten. If I'd known where you had settled, I wouldn't have had to search for you."

There was a silence between them. Silvie wiped a tear from her eye. She hadn't wanted to appear weak before her brother, but her emotions, the weariness, had taken control of her. Aoki shifted uneasily and looked away for a moment. Then he let his arms drop to his sides and his head slumped.

"I'm sorry, Silvie," he whispered. "You're right. You are my sister. The same blood flows in your veins as it does in mine. Since mother and father passed, we've only had each other. Maybe I was selfish to go out into the world by myself. If not, I was at least selfish in not informing you as to where I was. In your hour of need, I should have been there for you. By the spirit of Kami, I should have been there during the attack."

He walked over to her and sat down on the cot. The entire thing sunk below their combined weight.

"There was nothing you could have done, Aoki." Silvie placed her hand on his arm. "Instead, you might have died at the claws of those creatures. Like Tekasun, Sungi, and Naito."

"They're all dead." It wasn't a question, more of a resigned statement.

"Yes, and I cursed your name while I walked this land, searching for you." Silvie smiled. "But I found you, and we are now together."

"True." Aoki smiled back. "It's good to see you again, sister."

He embraced her, and she breathed in his smell. It all flooded back to her. All the memories she had forgotten or had displaced.

She wept again.

CHAPTER
SIX

Aoki left his sister to sleep in solitude. He had remained in her room until she closed her eyes, then he put out the candle next to her and snuck out. He joined Asari so that they could continue their vigil throughout the night.

Silvie could not sleep, though. Every time she

closed her eyes, the visions of dragons flying overhead, fire raining down onto the Golden Valley, the screams of dying kitsunes cutting through the smoke of burning buildings, all haunted her. But she couldn't rush to tell Aoki. No, she couldn't give him a reason to abandon his post.

WHEN THE LARGE DRAGONS APPEARED OUT OF THE mist, she had frozen. That was her first problem. She clasped her blade in a fugue state, simply staring at the dragon in front of her, flanked by several others. It hung there, suspended. The only things moving were the hideous wings that swayed back and forth in the silent breeze of the early morning.

Tekasun had pulled her from the state of delirium just in time for a pinpoint accurate flame to roar past her. As she lied there on the parapet, she looked down onto the valley below. The ground was covered with green creatures running toward the walls on all fours. They looked like dragons, but without wings and were much smaller, like a mix between a dragon and a human. They were a hideous blend, impossible for her to comprehend. They scaled the walls, coming closer and closer. And Silvie got up on her feet and beat them off with her blade, cutting at them, but with no luck.

"They are like dragons!" Naito called out. "Aim for their soft bellies to kill them."

She did so, cutting deep into an attacking beast, slicing it from side to side. Black blood poured from the creature as it crashed down behind her. The kitsunes continued to stand their ground, refusing to break the line, but the overwhelming number of enemies began to take its toll, and as night fell, the line broke.

Weak and weary, Silvie came to stand by Tekasun.

"This is too much," she told him. "We have to regroup or do something. The city behind us is already on fire, and we are losing warriors at an alarming rate."

"We stand our ground," he said after looking at Naito, who had given him a stern look.

She nodded and returned to the fight.

Tekasun had sent her away just as he was engulfed in flames and disintegrated. He'd told her to flee, to save herself, and find a safe haven.

"I will not abandon my post!" she screamed at him over the horrible sound of wood burning and kitsunes screaming.

"You must!" he called back to her. "One of us must survive."

No sooner after he had spoken those words, a dragon swooped down and batted him to the side. He crashed into the wall, temporarily losing consciousness. The giant beast roared in triumph. Silvie looked around. Sungi came up to her side, and they stared at each other.

"These big ones can be killed as well," Sungi said and swung her blade, stained with black blood. "Look!"

She pointed her weapon down toward the valley below. Two large bodies of dragons laid splayed across the ground. One of them impaled on the spire of the temple, the gold covered in the tar-like substance that the dragon used for blood.

"Then we take this bastard out as well." Silvie nodded. "We have to save Tekasun."

Sungi nodded back, and they both charged at the thing.

"We flank it!" Sungi cried out.

She charged for the head of the dragon, while Silvie flew in from behind. They both batted away the smaller looking dragons that they met along the way. The larger dragon watched Sungi closely as she swung for its head. But she couldn't quite reach it as it kept dodging her attempts. Silvie swung along the dragon's tail, moving toward the flailing head. Sungi used her stick and moved as she darted around in front of the dragon. The beast attempted to catch her, mighty jaws snapping where she was, missing her time after time again.

Silvie waited between the wings, crouching and

waiting to pounce. Her thighs burned as she tensed the muscles in them. They had been fighting all day, and the battle did not seem to be stopping any time soon. The two hundred kitsunes who once stood on the parapet were now down to perhaps fifty, and constantly dwindling.

Suddenly, the dragon slammed down one of its large claws, trapping Sungi beneath it like a cage. The momentary halt in movement from the dragon was the opportunity that Silvie needed. She leaped with all the strength her legs could muster, and she flew through the air toward the back of the skull, pointing the tip of her weapon toward the base of its head.

However, the point bounced off a scale, and the weapon slid from her hands. With horror, she watched as the blade flew through the air. The dragon jerked, and Silvie followed her weapon as she flew after it. She watched as the beast stepped down on top of Sungi, crushing her completely.

There was no time to react, and she landed hard on the parapet. She rolled over onto her side, only to find that she had landed next to the mutilated body of General Naito. She looked into his dead eyes, his mouth twisted into a horrible grimace. Silvie bit her lip and rolled over once more. She still needed to save Tekasun from being crushed also.

The shadow of the dragon cast her world into darkness, but she ran toward it, ignoring the pain in her body and the burn in her muscles. She picked up the blade in one swift movement and came sliding onto her knees under the belly of the beast.

It had hovered upon Tekasun again, sending several shots into his lifeless body. With the remaining strength she could muster, she plunged the cold steel into the soft tissue, instantly showered with warm, black liquid as the dragon bellowed in pain.

It took off into the air, twisting then crashing in the distance.

Silvie slowly rose to her feet and headed toward Tekasun. With tired eyes, he looked at her.

"Come with me," she said desperately. "We can flee and fight another day."

"You go, Silvie," he said hoarsely. He was still alive. "I am not going to make it. Just run. Save yourself and avenge us."

He closed his eyes and exhaled a ragged breath. His final one. With fury, she turned and headed back to the battle. She was mauled, scorched, stabbed, and scratched until she could barely walk anymore. She fell over the edge of the wall, toward the soft bodies piled below. She survived the fall and slowly walked away from the fight, the wails and cries still echoing behind her.

She had done as Tekasun commanded. Ran to the hills, turned, and watched as her home turned into ruins. Then a great red dragon, larger than she'd ever seen before, landed on the city wall, completely shattering it.

She headed south. To the only family or friend she knew. Her brother. Weak from the battle and injuries that she had sustained, she trudged on. The change in weather didn't make it any easier, and she tried to nurse her wounds the best she could.

THERE WAS A TEMPORARY LULL IN THE STORM raging outside, and she decided that tossing and turning on the cot wasn't getting her anywhere. She got up and climbed the stairs of the watchtower and out onto the widow's walk at the top. She was in the eye of the storm. Standing in the stillness while the world raged around her on all sides. She watched the South Sea roil below, a natural defense against any potential attackers.

"Can't sleep?" Asari came up behind her.

"Too much on my mind," Silvie replied and leaned against the railing. "I keep playing the attack over and over in my head. As if there were something I could have done to stop it, or save my comrades."

She touched the eagle crest on her chest.

"I understand." Asari came to stand next to her. "We are trained to keep after our brothers and sisters, and I understand if you feel guilty that they were left behind."

"They were all basically dead by the time I fled," Silvie said. "But if I could have saved the few who remained, we would have a stronger fighting force."

"There is no time for regret," Asari explained. "You are here with us now, and that is all that matters."

"It's not about regret. I'm more so afraid that it will happen again," Silvie said. "I've missed you, Asari." She smiled coyly.

"It *has* been years, despite what Aoki believes." He smiled back. "Remember how we used to play below this tower? Challenging each other to get close to the cliff, to avoid the waves and riptides?"

"I do." She looked back out over the water. "Aoki is much too young to remember."

"I think something pulled him here all the same." Asari sighed. "Like a distant, hidden memory of happy times."

"The days before the displacement." Silvie joined his sigh. "Sorry for not keeping in contact with you."

"Don't worry." Asari placed a hand on her shoulder. "It works both ways. I could have sent you letters or come to visit."

"I'm here now." She looked him deep in the eyes. "What's been happening in your life?"

"Since you left for the valley?" Asari smiled. "Where do I begin?"

CHAPTER
SEVEN

As days continued to pass, the inclement weather seemed to keep the dragons away from the southern region. Reports flooded in from all surrounding areas of other attacks, of dragons annihilating cities and villages. There were also rumors of onis and other beasts ravaging the remains of the villages, but it didn't seem like they were part of the dragons' plans. Instead, they appeared to be byproducts of the attacks. Dragons would just as likely kill the onis or kappas without remorse.

At first, Silvie thought that the smaller dragons *were* a product of oni-dragon mating, but that was apparently not the case. As time passed, they received more and more reports of nomadic tribes of onis being slaughtered by roaming bands of dragons, especially in the foothills of the northern mountains and the great rice fields in the west.

Surviving kitsunes flooded Preserve, seeking refuge. Warriors were greeted with open arms while others became increasingly difficult to place in the limited space within the city walls.

Silvie joined the Preserve warriors, and it felt good to take part in the drills again. When she and Asari were not on watch, they spent time together in the Inner Sanctum, an elaborate garden below the city. This was also where the Eagles gathered to discuss the defenses of the city. Very much like the gardens around the temple in the Golden Valley, this was also where the elders gathered.

Yet it seemed as if the elders in Preserve were more invisible than they had been in Silvie's village. She thought she had seen one or two, dressed in elaborate silk kimonos with gilded embroidery, out of the corner of her eye, but when she tried to take a closer look, they were gone.

The Eagles called a meeting of the assembled kitsune warrior tribes. There were Wolves, Badgers, Bears, and Ravens, to name a few, but Silvie was the only Fox, and it stung her heart to feel so alone. The remaining commanders of each clan sat in a lotus position on the ground, weapons across their knees.

"Once the season turns, the dragons will attack us," Aoki said. "I don't believe that is a secret to anyone."

"Agreed," Asari replied and looked at the assembled commanders. "But we have an advantage now. We now have an assemblage of kitsunes from all corners of the world, and with that, the accumulated knowledge of several attacks. Together, we can surmise how the dragons will attack us, and thus, be prepared."

"I understand that we all have experiences," Tanahashi, one of the Badgers, spoke up. "But do we have time to amass all this knowledge before the dragons come?"

"I believe we do," Asari replied. "All our cities and villages were located at different places in the Far East."

"So?" Cima, one of the Ravens, asked.

"This gives us a clear advantage," Asari replied. "Cima, your city was high in the mountains, which forced the dragons to rely more on flight. Tanahashi, your village was on an island along the East Sea, which in turn, forced the dragons to utilize the water. It taught us how long they could stay elevated for. The Golden Valley was protected by high walls, Silvie." He looked at her. "This forced the smaller dragons to use their talons to scale. It all comes together in a beautiful packet of information."

"And this could all be used to defeat them," Aoki added. "May Kami now protect and help us against this foe."

The commanders all murmured in agreement, and then they rose to leave.

"Let us split into groups to best utilize what we have now," Silvie suggested before they all scattered.

This time, there was a murmur of disapproval. The kitsunes were not known for their cooperative abilities, but they reluctantly split into working groups, each one with its own range of competence.

AS THE WIND DIED DOWN, AND THE HOURS OF sunlight became more bountiful, they prepared the walls and trained their warriors. Asari kept Silvie close by. He used the guise of picking her brain as it pertained to the dragon movement and attack patterns, but in truth, he had grown fond of her and just wanted to be near her.

And Silvie didn't turn down the invites, joining him as they walked the perimeters of the city walls, or along the cliff they used to play at as children. She eagerly watched as large vessels were pushed out into the water in strategic positions to catch any unguarded dragons.

"According to our scouts," Asari said as they stood at the newly enforced city gates, "the dragons are circling Preserve and should be here within the week."

"It feels as if a noose is tightening around our necks," Silvie replied, "like we must be on our toes at every waking moment."

"It's part of their tactic," Asari said and stared out over the open plains of the southern region. "They deprive us of sleep, and then they attack."

"Well, it looks like we'll be ready for them." Silvie smiled at him, then suddenly, slipped her hand into his. "I just want you to know, Asari, that if something were to happen to either of us, that I have come to grow very fond of our time together."

"I agree, Silvie," he replied, looked deep into her eyes, and squeezed her hand. "I have become more than fond of you."

He leaned in and kissed her gently.

Suddenly, the entire tower shook. Silvie jumped in

shock and instinctively reached for the blade she had carelessly dropped onto the ground. Another hit rattled the structure, and this time, it roused Asari.

"They're here!" he screamed. "Time to man the walls."

They both leaped from the bed in his quarters and quickly got dressed, in the manner they had practiced several times before, and then slipped into their kimonos and armor with ease. They headed out into the hubbub of the early morning. They had come to the conclusion that the dragons mostly attacked at dawn, or as close to it as possible, so they were ready.

Scores of kitsune warriors from all tribes were running to their stations, not a single one unprepared as to where they needed to be in that very moment. Some manned the large arbalests, giant crossbows mounted at intervals, and began aiming them into the dark. Others lit large pyres all around them to light up the night sky, in order to make it easier to see the enemy. Archers took up their positions, while foot soldiers formed lines below.

The dragons came from all sides. Scorched the ground with their flames in long fiery runnels toward the outer wall of Preserve. The kitsunes had coated the stone with a thick layer of flame-retardant paint that was supposed to keep the fire from damaging it. Blast after blast shot against the stone, only to run off like water on a goose.

The dragons roared in frustration. They needed to break down the walls in order for their smaller counterparts to get into the city proper. They couldn't scale the walls, either, for the warriors had made sure that the walls had no cracks or crevices to use for climbing.

Once the dragons noticed this, they simply brought in the larger dragons, with their blue flames, more intense and hotter. They landed on the ground in front of the main wall, and with one unified flame, shot straight at it.

It melted the stone, bringing the first wall down, exposing the second one. This wall was craggier, and the smaller dragons could easily scale them. They were met by the kitsune warriors with steel and fury. Silvie heard the clanging of blades against scales, the awful sound of claws tearing into flesh, and the wet sound of blood being spilled. Cries of dying kitsunes were intermingled with the gurgling of dragons crying out.

The dragons then started dropping boulders from their claws, making it rain on the homes below, crushing them in the process. Kitsunes fled out onto the streets, only to be crushed in the aftermath. Silvie could see both young and elderly kitsunes falling below the hail of rocks, heads crushed under the blunt force.

The archers proceeded to fire arrows straight up

into the air. A few dragons were hit, both by arbalest arrows and the smaller ones. They crashed to the ground, spitting up large chunks of dirt and crushing some of the smaller dragons. Every time a dragon fell, the gathered crowd cheered, but the jubilation was short lived when another dragon took its place.

The ships on the water were no match for the beasts, who simply hovered above them, flapping their leathery wings and creating vortexes of air that toppled the vessels. Some of the arrows managed to hit one or two of the enemy, but other than that, the ships were of no use at all.

Aoki, Asari, and Silvie stood shoulder to shoulder, fighting off the smaller wingless dragons who now started to climb the wall. Their sharp blades took down their enemy one by one, cutting through their soft bellies. The ground was slick with black, putrid blood, and they were finding it difficult to keep themselves from slipping.

Still, they held the line as best they could, but it was become increasingly difficult to keep the onslaught at bay. Fire rose from the burning city behind them, and with that, the dying screams of kitsunes, both young and old.

The smoke surrounded them, making it harder to breathe and see. Silvie had to turn and listen for the clicks of taloned feet on the ground for the next attack.

Once the sound ceased, she would see a dark shadow come from the smoke, and she'd turn, blade in hand, cutting the attacker down in a spray of dark blood.

"This isn't going to hold!" Aoki screamed as he pierced another enemy.

"Stand your ground!" Asari shouted back while doing the same.

"We need a plan," Silvie responded. "We need to advance somehow, and get out of the smoke."

"I agree," Asari said. "We have to move forward in order to get a clearer view of the situation. Maybe even catch the dragons from behind."

"Why don't I take a group of warriors and circle around?" Aoki shouted. "If the dragons notice that they are being attacked from the rear, they might shift their focus, and we can advance."

"Good plan," Silvie replied.

Aoki began moving, trying to gather the stray warriors close to them.

Then suddenly, one of the dragons burst out from the smoke and speared Silvie, pushing her body back with such force that she lost her breath. The scaled shoulder felt hard against her abdomen as it brought her down with full force against the cold, hard walk. Asari tried to get the beast off her, but was soon overpowered by beasts of his own.

Silvie and the dragon rolled around, both jockeying

for position, when the creature suddenly howled. It placed a taloned hand on her face, and she could smell the stench of death upon it. The dragon then howled again, and a larger one came down from the gray sky. The smaller dragon released her as the larger one grabbed her body with its claws and alighted.

Asari screamed as he watched the dragon fly away with her limp body. She looked down, only to see a familiar sight. Preserve was on fire. The village crushed by large boulders and completely overrun by dragons on the ground. All the ships had sunk, bodies of drowned kitsunes bobbing on the waves. The walls were torn down, and the great towers still standing were caught in a blazing fire.

But eventually, the dizzying height caused her to pass out. Another failed defense was the last thing she could see.

EIGHT

Silvie was cold. She was shivering and cold. It was dark as well. She was shrouded in darkness, moving her hands around her to feel for anything familiar. There was straw under her, and beneath that, stone. Cold, wet stone. Silvie rolled over onto her back and allowed her vision to adjust to the darkness.

Slowly, she sat up and looked around. She was in some sort of cavern, surrounded by sharp, jagged rocks. A cool breeze wafted through what must be a series of tunnels running through the caves. She thought she could hear the whimpers and cries from creatures bouncing off the walls in the cave.

She blinked a few times. Kitsune eyes were very well-equipped to the dark, but this seemed to be some magical dimness that she was having trouble overcoming. She sat up and moved with her back to the wall along a small passage, crouching in order to avoid detection. Her body still ached, and she had no real sense of how long she had been held captive. She'd passed out quickly after becoming airborne.

She could have been here for several days, hours, or even just minutes. If she were to go by the pain in her body, she would say a mere couple of hours, but it was really difficult to tell. Gently, she moved along the wall. She thought she could see shapes in the darkness but was unsure. They might as well have been various crags or outcroppings shaped as bodies.

Carefully, she felt her way around one of the corners from where some yellow light had emanated. The whimpering she'd heard before grew more intense. She peeked her head around to find one of the smaller dragons, the foot soldiers, like the one that had speared her, writhing in pain on the ground. Torches hung on the wall of the open area in which it dwelled, and as it rolled around, the dragon's shadow moved in an angry dance.

Silvie felt a pang of sympathy for the brown, scaly creature. With taloned hands, it clutched its soft yellow belly. It cried, rows of sharp teeth snapping in the air. Even though this was the enemy, the destroyer of her world, she wanted to comfort it. The beast looked so vulnerable and sad. It pulled at her heartstrings.

"Don't," a ragged voice said in the dark.

"What?" Silvie replied to the voice.

"It is transforming," a fae slid into the yellow light. "That beast was once human. Kidnapped as we were, and now morphing into one of the dragon's minions."

It was an older fae. His hair had turned silver, wisps of hair around his mouth and on his pointy ears, and his eyes were slightly milky. Silvie thought it might be a dryad, but it was very difficult to tell in the dark.

"Are you telling me—" Silvie began.

"That those small ones are not true dragons?" the aged fae interrupted. "I have been here long enough to see many humans, faes, and onis alike come into these caves and get turned into dragonmites."

"How does it happen?" Silvie observed the writhing creature.

"The dragons have devised some sort of concoction from ancient fruits and berries found within these caves." The aged one patted the damp wall behind him. "This is where they were trapped. In these caves below the Dragon Isles, forged long ago by the Dragon Lord, who wasn't a god but acted like one."

"The dragons were biding their time," Silvie filled in. "Building up an army of dragonmites that they could sacrifice at will."

"Indeed." The aged one looked down. "This would allow them to rule the known world, and maybe beyond."

Silvie turned from the aged fae to the dragonmite. "What do we do?" she asked.

"These blossoms." The fae held out his hand to reveal the heads of red flowers. "They are found here on the island. Eat them, and the effects of the concoction is reversed. It may serve to one day bring down the dragons, but how? I do not know."

He dropped them onto the ground, allowing them to slowly float down against the breeze moving through the cave. Then he vanished back into the dark.

Silvie didn't say a word. She knew from experience that old kitsunes became reclusive and strange with time, but the story he told seemed too far-fetched to now be true. She picked up the flowers and slipped them into the sleeve of her kimono.

As she prepared herself to find a way to escape, the dragonmite howled in pain. It cut her to the core, and she felt like she couldn't possibly leave the creature alone.

Silently, she scooted into the opening, carefully approaching the thing.

"Excuse me," she whispered.

The dragonmite paused, but she could still see the pain on its scaly face. It cocked its head sideways to look at her with yellow eyes and grunted.

"My name is Silvie," she continued.

"Kitsune?" the thing growled, throat and mouth struggling with pronouncing such delicate words.

"Yes, that's right," she replied. "Who are you?"

"I..." It paused and thought for a moment. "I think my name is Arashi. Maybe."

"The transformation must be affecting your memory," Silvie said. "How long have you been here?"

"A dragon brought me," the dragonmite began. "Not long ago. They fed me before the pain came."

Arashi looked at his hands. "Something is different," he said. "These look different."

Silvie sympathized with the poor creature. She could almost see the human side of him beneath all the scales. There was something in its eyes, maybe the last shred of its humanity.

THERE WERE TUNNELS. LONG AND DARK TUNNELS that led down below the rocks. They twisted like a spiral staircase into the belly of the island, far beneath the surface of the South Sea. If one dared to continue in the utter blackness, one would soon encounter glimmering rocks.

They would be part of the foundation, glowing and lighting the way further down. The walls pockmarked with holes that served as air vents to prevent death by suffocation.

The glimmering was all part of the magic on the island, created when it was formed eons ago. This was what kept the island hidden from travelers passing by. Located in the middle of the South Sea, it would naturally be in the way of any trading ships headed to the south, yet no sailor had ever discovered it.

Some would speak of a strange, eerie sensation looming over them as they passed a certain point on the sea. Like the hairs on the nape of their neck standing on edge, coupled with a strange humming sound that permeated across the surface of the water. There was an enchantment over the island, hiding it from view. Like a haze making it diffuse, it was always out of focus. A keen eye might spot something in the distance or out of the corner of their vision, but it would always be gone if focused on. Ships also automatically swerved past it without control, as if the island made sure to avoid a crash on its shores.

Once, a human had walked the entire length of the labyrinthine passage, sometimes crawling on his belly in order to fit, and he reached a great cave. In this cave, there was a lake, a dark body of water of a tar-like substance akin to the blood that flowed in the dragons' veins. And in the center of this lake was an island, similar to the Dragon Isle itself. A miniature version of the home of the dragons.

On this island, sat the Dragon Lord. His body covering the entire land mass, claws resting atop the jagged rocks, while his head rested on a mountain range.

He appeared to be sleeping. His eyes were closed while his breath came in short, measured intervals. Smoke slowly curling from his great nostrils, the serpentine body wrapped around the rock, gently squeezing it so that it partly crumbled.

He never showed himself to anyone, apart from one of the dragons. The commander of his army, the one that listened to him and took his orders. Otherwise, he haunted dragons and dragonmites alike in their dreams. He taunted them, filled them with images of hatred, of humans and faes torturing their kind. It filled them with hatred. The exact thing he needed them to feel in order to bring about chaos to the Far East and propagate his agenda, to kill the children of the deities who had denied him access to their realm.

He had formed the island as a sanctuary. A place for him to create his offspring and hone their skills. Where he taught the first ones to fly, to breath fire, and to kill. He sent them out across the sea to attack the homes of all the creatures of the Far East, all his enemies. They had proven to be stronger than he'd imagined. They had created tactics, weapons, forged metal, and built homes out of stone and wood instead of reconstructing nature out of magic. They had fought back, and his creations had not been able to withstand it in the end.

Like him, they were ornery and vile. Hated everything, even other dragons, and it made it difficult to organize them. The humans, the vile Kurata's children, formed special dragon-killing warriors who sought them out and slayed them.

The Dragon Lord retreated and meditated on the problem. One dragon was easy enough to defeat, but if he could make them co-operate, they would be a strong force to reckon with. For centuries, he hid, forming new dragons, teaching them to co-exist. To form unified attacks, and thus, he created the commander who would be his voice, his direct link to the dragons. When the time was right, he'd be ready to strike, and he knew where to do it. He wanted to strike at their heart, at the biggest threat, at Kami's pride and joy. The kitsunes.

So, he set his sights on the impenetrable Golden Valley. If it were to fall, the dragons would be proven unstoppable.

"I will stop at nothing," Asari said as he looked down upon the ruins that had once been Preserve.

"What can we do?" Kota, from the Wolves tribe, asked. "The dragons have shown us that they are more powerful than we could've ever imagined."

The Wolves belonged to a northern Kitsune clan.

They were fierce in battle, unafraid, but also without caution. The Foxes didn't care for their reckless ways, but it produced results, and in the end, a fair number of dragons had been struck down due to the sacrifices of many dead Wolves.

"Everyone has a weakness," Asari replied. "Even the dragons, and I intend to figure out what it is."

"But we don't have enough fighters left to even attempt an attack," Aoki said.

"We send runners to all corners of this land, and they'll carry messages from us. A call to arms and join us in battle. This time, we call on all the races. Onis, kitsunes, and humans. We need everyone here to defeat the dragons," Asari instructed.

"What if the onis are allies of the dragons?" Kota asked. "These small dragon-like beings could just be the onis, but in a new shape. Like the abysmal kappas."

"That is a chance we must take," Asari said. "There have been reports, albeit few, that the dragons have killed the onis as well, but I don't know if that's true."

"I would be completely certain of this before we initiate contact with any oni," a gray mustached kitsune said.

It was one of the Preserve elders. His gilded kimono was in rags as he stood on the ruins of what used to be his temple. Asari and Aoki took a knee while

Kota remained standing. It had become a tradition among the kitsunes not to venerate elders from other clans. It made little sense, but had become a way to differentiate one group from another. It was not what Kami had wanted when she created them, but it seemed to be a natural progression in the ultra-competitive world of the faes.

"Elder Yoshino," Asari said, surprise. "I am thrilled to see you alive."

"It is not because of the defense of the Eagles, I am afraid." The elder fae looked down at them with contempt.

Asari rose and said, "The odds were stacked against us. We did our best."

"I suppose so." Yoshino descended from the rubble. "Are there enough kitsunes to take out this dreaded threat before we all become extinct?"

"Elder Yoshino." Aoki rose as well. "We will do everything in our power to defeat the enemy and its allies."

"I would venture out into the universe to find warriors instead of sending runners." Yoshino came to stand before Asari. "There is a heavy burden on your shoulders now, Eagle. Make us proud."

Yoshino walked past him and continued through the ruins of his once proud home. Asari looked at the elder from behind with tears in his eyes. He didn't know what pained him more: the disappointment in Yoshino's voice, the task now placed upon him, or the loss of Silvie.

OTHER DRAGONMITES WANDERED THROUGH THE caves. Most of them had completed their transformations and could barely speak. They brought food and water, and at various intervals, even a brownish liquid that Silvie assumed was the concoction. She silently poured it out onto the straw when they weren't looking at her.

When they stood on their hind legs and monitored her, she closed her eyes and downed the odious drink, then as soon as the guard vanished toward other prisoners, she grabbed a flower and placed it into her mouth.

Time passed, and she remained by Arashi's side as he seemed to vanish more and more into the haziness of oblivion. She tried to keep the process at bay by feeding him flowers, but it seemed that his body was too deep into the transformation. When he slept, she snuck around, attempting to find a way out.

She came upon an opening that led to green rolling hills atop cliffs that overlooked a raging sea. A field of the red flowers stretched out before her, and she replenished her stock of the natural antidote. Before returning, she looked out over the sea, imagining that she could see the mainland in the distance. Something had changed inside her, though. She had lost the sense of longing, and instead, felt only contempt for the creatures that must live on the other side of the water.

She frowned at it. What was happening to her? Did she even care what it might be? She felt the pull from inside the cave and desperately wanted to be with Arashi. It was a familiar feeling, one that she had felt before, but not toward the dragonmite, toward someone else. But who? There was a sensation that there was something else out there for her, or someone else.

She shook her head and headed back into the cave with her blossoms.

"You are losing yourself," the aged one said as he sat down beside Silvie in the darkness.

She leaned against the cold cave wall, head resting against one of the jagged rocks. Arashi slept beside her, his breath coming in shallow bursts. His transformation was all but complete, and the pain had subsided. She placed her hand on his thigh, feeling the warmth through his scaly skin.

"What do you mean?" she asked in a tired voice.

"You have allowed the darkness within the dragons to seep into your soul," the fae replied. "Once the concoction takes hold of the body and mind, the evil that is inside may infect those close by."

"You are speaking like a crazy fae, aged one," Silvie said with a vile tone. "This place and your solitude have destroyed your mind."

"Have they?" he replied. "I have seen kitsunes and humans alike land on this island, and those who do not transform into dragonmites, those who refuse the concoction somehow, become tainted by the curse of the dragons."

"You know not of what you speak," Silvie retorted and waved him away. "If this were true, how come you haven't gone mad?"

"Because I am older and more powerful," he said and moved closer to her. "I can withstand what you cannot." He placed his hands on her chest. "Believe me," he pleaded. "Don't let it take you. Remove yourself from this thing, this creature who was once human."

She pushed him away, but the aged one came back to her. Once again, grabbing her by the tattered kimono.

"Let it go!" he cried to her.

"Release me!" she cried back and slapped him hard across his face.

He continued to hold on, and she continued to slap him until he went down on one knee. She put her hands around his throat and began to choke him. His milky eyes grew wide, and his tongue protruded from his mouth as he let out a low gargle and sank to the ground.

Silvie stood above the lifeless body of one of her own and smiled. The familiar call to arms echoed through the cave as the dragons prepared for another attack. Arashi stirred. This would be his first battle as a dragonmite, and she would join him. She would fight for the dragons against their treacherous foe.

CHAPTER

TEN

ON THE ISLET OF ELMWOOD, A STREAM FLOWED, wide and deep with cold water from the northern mountains. It was the home of the naiads, faes who lived in cold water more than they lived on land. They had no issues living on land, but preferred the sanctuary of the liquid element. Their villages were partly submerged. Buildings were made from impregnated wood that would not rot when constantly in water. Some of their holier buildings, such as temples and more official structures, were properly underneath the water.

Asari and Aoki wandered onto the wide open field that was basically only grass with a wide stream flowing through it. To differentiate themselves from the dryads, naiads had cut down all the trees in the area. It had been a way for them to ensure the dominance of their territory. Even if the dryads could venture outside the dense vegetation of the woods, they rarely did. Just as the naiads were less than eager to wander too far away from water.

"I have never been too fond of this area," Aoki told Asari and held a hand on the hilt of his weapon.

"These wide open spaces make us prone to an ambush," Asari agreed. "From dragons, naiads, or even wild animals."

Further down the stream, they saw a figure sitting on a collection of rocks. Something like a dam that the naiads had created to catch fish, their main source of food. Further away, they could see the first glimpse of structures that must surely be homes. The Eagles, who lived on the southern coast, rarely ventured inland anymore, which was where most of the other faes lived, so they were inexperienced when it came to interactions with others.

"Whoa!" Asari cried out and raised a hand to show that he wasn't holding his weapon.

"I would've snuck up on it instead," Tanahashi, who had joined them, said. "This leaves us at their mercy."

"They have no reason to distrust us," Aoki said and shot him a sideways glance. "Is that not what we all do?" he asked.

"Distrust one another?" Tanahashi asked.

"Do you not distrust me the way I distrust other kitsunes or faes?"

"I suppose I do." Tanahashi looked around. "But in the past, we never had a reason to trust each other. Now all of a sudden, we are going to. It is all well and good when it comes to the same races, like kitsunes, but naiads, humans, or onis, that is another thing entirely."

"If we are going to succeed in defeating the enemy," Asari turned and looked at them, "then we need to see past the differences that separate us, and focus on what makes us the same."

"And what would that be?" Aoki scoffed.

"I have yet to figure that out." Asari turned on his heel again and headed to the figure on the rocks.

"What have we here?" one of naiads asked as she slid into the water, arms extended to stop her upper body from emersion.

She looked similar to a kitsune, but her skin was

darker. Her light brown hair had a similar tint as her body, which they could clearly see since she wore no clothes. She also had almond eyes, and her ears were pointed. She tapped her long pointy nails against the wet stone and sighed.

"We are looking for some kind of leader or commander," Asari answered. "I am Asari, of the Eagles."

"Kitsune, huh?" the naiad replied and clicked her tongue. "When the dragons rise from oblivion, the kitsunes come crawling."

"What's that supposed to mean?" Tanahashi snapped.

"I like him." The naiad nodded and winked at him with a wry smile. "Let him talk."

"Excuse me," Asari said. "But I'm the commander—"

"Naiads care not for chains of command," the naiad interrupted. "We govern ourselves the way we see fit. We bow to no one."

"So, you have no leader, then?" Aoki asked.

"The two of you bore me." She waved them away. "Let the grumpy one do the talking."

Asari and Aoki looked over at Tanahashi, who let his shoulders slump down as he shuffled toward the stream.

The naiad ducked into the water and emerged close to the bank, where the kitsune stood.

"Now, tell me," she said, "what can I do for you?"

"Well, you see—" Tanahashi began.

"Iko," the naiad interrupted again. "My name is Iko."

"Alright, Iko," he stammered. "It must not come as a surprise to you that the land has seen a rise of the dragons and their ilk."

"We would have to be deaf, dumb, *and* blind not to notice it," Iko mocked.

"Right." Tanahashi went on. "They recently destroyed Preserve, one of the last kitsune strongholds. After this happened, the remaining kitsunes gathered at where it once stood to create a unified attack on them. Find out where they live and strike it."

"That sounds like a noble venture," Iko replied. "What do you need from us?"

"We cannot do this alone," he replied. "We need the help of all the creatures in this universe. Combined. That means all faes, humans, and even the onis."

"Onis?" Iko threw her head back in laughter. "You think you can summon those hideous creatures and order them around?"

"We have nothing to lose—" Asari began, but Iko raised a slender finger.

"Nothing to lose?" she asked. "What about our lives and homes?"

"We are going to lose them, anyway," Tanahashi replied. "Do you truly believe that the dragons will leave you alone? They will come for you even if you refuse to stand with us. They will rain fire on this village as well. It doesn't matter to them if you stand idly by and do nothing while we attack."

Iko remained silent for a moment.

"The naiads may just be the missing puzzle piece we need to tip the scale," he pleaded. "There are skills you possess that may come in handy. Stand with us. For the good of this universe."

Iko pulled herself up from the river and climbed onto the grassy bank. The sunlight glittered off her naked body, and she shook her head from side to side to allow the excess water to shower the envoys of kitsunes.

"I agree," she finally said. "We can sit this one out and choose to not die on the battlefield, but that only means that the enemy will come to us. No matter when it happens, I am convinced that it will. The naiads will join in on this fight. Give us a few days to mobilize, and I shall gather the remaining tribes. We have also been decimated by the wrath of the dragons, and we know all too well what it's like to lose loved ones to their flames."

"You can give that order?" Tanahashi asked. "I thought the naiads followed no one."

"I lied," Iko said. "I am the chieftain of this tribe." She winked at him and walked closer, only to plant a kiss on his cheek. "By the way, you make a convincing argument, kitsune."

"Now this place makes me even more uncomfortable than the open field," Aoki said as they set foot into the deep dark woods.

They had traveled from the field of the naiads to deeper into the center of the land, called The Eye of the Far East. The Eye consisted of a dense wooded area filled with all types of shrubbery, trees, and bushes. It was a large area, almost stretching out for miles in each direction. It was also surrounded by a range of mountains, creating a controlled climate, making the region lush with vegetation.

"We are sitting ducks here, for sure," Asari replied. "Who knows what hides behind each dark corner and tall tree?"

"But we will also have the advantage over any enemy," Aoki said.

"True." Asari looked around, treading carefully over roots and branches.

"I think we get Tanahashi to negotiate with the dryads." Aoki looked at the third kitsune in the party. "He did such a great job with Iko."

"Get bent," Tanahashi said, and he pushed Aoki's back.

They continued to traverse deeper and deeper into the thicket, forced to use their blades to cut through it as they moved. While they walked, the noise from all the wildlife intensified and grew shriller, as if they feared the invaders coming into their domain.

A soft thud and the crack of branches could be heard all around them, and they looked around. Suddenly, they stood surrounded by four figures dressed in green tunics. They stood almost a foot taller than the kitsunes, with long red hair tied back into braids. Like the other faes, their eyes were almond shaped, their ears pointed, but they were pale. Unaccustomed to the rays of the sun, their skin was shaded by the dense crowns of the trees. They carried spears and bows with arrows notched.

"Dryads?" Asari asked and looked all around at their stern, emotionless faces.

"Kitsunes?" one of them replied and smiled.

"We are," Tanahashi said. He kept his hand on his weapon.

This caused the dryad to grip the spear tighter.

"There is no need for the rattle of weapons," Asari

said and raised his hands.

"Tell your friend," the dryad spoke again.

Asari looked over at Tanahashi and nodded. The kitsune agreed and relaxed his arms.

"My name is Asari, and this is Aoki and Tanahashi," Asari said. "We are looking for a leader among the dryads."

"My name is Akebono," the dryad said. "These are my sisters, Toru, Okamaru, and Naruki. We do have a leader, but for what reason do you wish to speak with her?"

"We are here to make an offer," Asari said.

"That being?" Naruki cut in.

"We want to form an alliance," Tanahashi said.

"An alliance for what?" Okamaru asked with a skeptical air. "There is nothing the kitsunes can offer us that we don't already have."

"We know the dragons have lain waste to most of the dryad settlements in the Far East, so from our standpoint, you do need help," Asari retorted.

"That's just your way of seeing things," Naruki replied. "But we've heard that the kitsunes are not doing any better."

"That's exactly why we're here," Asari said. "We are at least humble enough to admit when we need help."

"That wasn't always the case." Naruki smiled. "I

see it more as you've been humbled. The mighty sure have fallen since this war began."

"Look," Aoki cut in. "We didn't come all the way here to be insulted. The relationship between the dryads and the kitsunes has been a contentious one. We have killed enough of each other since the dawn of time, but this time, we need to come together and fight a common foe, if we are to survive."

"Don't come here crawling on your bellies and begging for our assistance." Naruki spat onto the ground. "We can manage the dragons on our own."

"Wait!" Akebono raised a hand to silence the agitated Naruki. "Let me have a word, please. It is true that the hardest battles among the faes have been between the kitsunes and the dryads. We have battled back and forth, back and forth. I have done my fair share of killing, and so have you, Asari. Yes, I know who you are and the fierce foe you can be, but no matter how much I might detest you, it doesn't change the fact that we, the dryads, have suffered from the attacks." She pointed at her spear over to the west. "In our city, Petrified Springs, we are now hosting legions of dryads who have lost their homes and family members. We know how it feels to suffer."

"Akebono?" Naruki looked stunned.

"Silence, Naruki!" Akebono roared.

She moved swiftly and placed the point of the

spear at the throat of her fellow dryad. Pinning her body to the trunk of a tree with her own body.

"You don't know what it's like to greet a sister," she snarled. "Standing at your doorstep in tatters, dirty, and with tears streaming down a sooty face. Telling you that her entire family has succumbed to the flames of flying lizards."

Naruki shuddered with fear at the rage of Akebono, and Aoki thought that the dryad would truly run through her friend. There was a long pause, and then Akebono released Naruki.

"You have been sitting here safe and sound." Akebono lowered the spear, but then pointed a finger at Naruki. "Your loved ones are still alive. So, you don't know. I say we take them to the queen. Anyone want to oppose that decision?" She moved the spear from dryad to dryad, and none of them said anything. "Didn't think so."

Akebono turned to the gathered kitsunes and gestured with her head where they should go. Asari nodded a reply and began walking. He saw a path that he hadn't noticed before, and they headed down it. The dryads took the back of the train to keep an eye on them.

Aoki couldn't help but think about the words of Akebono. About her sister coming to her on a rainy night with that fear in her eyes. That sadness and the disappointment she must've felt at not being able to be there in her hour of need. He knew how Akebono must feel about it, even though he might not know why these dryad siblings were ever apart from one another.

The trees were growing thicker and thicker as they moved deeper and deeper into the woods, until they arrived at a glade with tall, thick trees that formed a circle.

They could clearly see rope bridges running between the branches. Large wooden structures acted as homes, temples, shops, or whatever was necessary for a functioning village. They could smell the delicious fragrance of food cooking, hear the sound of a blacksmith, and even the laughter of children. It made them all miss what had once been their homes.

It took the breath out of Aoki when he saw so much joy, but he could also sense a feeling of fear, maybe trepidation at what might eventually come.

The party walked toward the center of the circle, where Akebono motioned for them to halt. She looked around at the crowd that had gathered around the strangers. Then she raised her head and let out a strange call. It sounded almost like a joyful bird call, but not like any bird Asari had ever heard.

Immediately at the sound, a rope came down from the tallest tree, where a palace-like structure dwelled. Once the end of the rope touched the ground, a dryad, dressed in a white cloak, slid down. The figure's hood was up, so it obscured the face of the person whom Asari soon realized was the aforementioned queen. She was dressed in all white, from her boots to the leggings and tunic that he could see underneath the cloak. Green trim decorated the edges of the clothes, giving it a deeper look. Akebono came close to her and whispered something to the hood, and then moved over to the side.

The queen removed her cloak to reveal a beautiful face with sharp lines and clear green eyes. Her hair was also tied up in an elaborate braid, which hung down her left side.

"So, it is an alliance you are looking for?" she asked.

"That is true, queen." Asari bowed his head, as did Tanahashi and Aoki.

"You may call me Hamada," the queen said. "We are informal, so titles are unnecessary."

"Well, then, Hamada," Asari smiled, "we are looking for allies against the threat of the dragons."

"An alliance?" Hamada thought about it for a moment. "I assume that such an alliance already exists in part. Who are your current allies?"

"All the last clans of kitsunes and the naiads," Tanahashi cut in.

"Then we are not the last ones in line." Hamada looked at the new speaker.

"I suppose not," Asari said. "Although, we have yet to decide who we are approaching next."

"I would suggest that an alliance against the dragons cannot survive without the humans." Hamada looked over to the side.

"Or the onis," Aoki added.

"That is also true." She looked at him. "Both the onis and the humans possess abilities and powers that we do not. The onis are tenacious while the humans aggressive. This could be a powerful combination that would serve us well."

"So, you are with us, then?" Asari felt surprised at the ease of it all.

"I have waited for this day ever since the attack on the Golden Valley," she replied. "But I was too afraid to approach the other faes or creatures, even to broach the topic. Afraid of being laughed at, or even killed in the process."

"What reason do you have to be afraid?" Aoki asked.

"Because we have been at war with each other for long enough, that a stranger showing up in search of a truce is as close as being dead upon arrival."

"But your warriors did not kill us," Asari said.

"Times are different now." Hamada bit her lip. "We need all the soldiers we can get. We will come with you on this journey."

CHAPTER
ELEVEN

Kitsunes were bred to be brave. Nothing was supposed to scare them, not even rattle them in the heat of a battle. When the dragons attacked, Asari felt no fear at all, even when the towers came crashing down, or when he realized that they were going to lose.

Approaching the dryads, naiads, or the other faes on their travels didn't frighten him, either. In the end, they were all like distant cousins to him, and even if they lived a different life, worshipped other gods, and resided in homes that were foreign to the kitsunes, there was always a hint of recognition. Something familiar, either in architecture, speech patterns, or clothing. It made him and his traveling companions feel safe.

As the days turned into weeks, and the weeks turned into months, they had almost covered the entire Far East, and every living kitsune joined them. It gave him a sense of pride, that they had managed to achieve the impossible, but the next challenge would be more trying.

If he had trained away the fear as a young kitsune, it returned to him now. It came back like an unwelcomed friend as they stood on one of the seven hills that surrounded the humans' capital.

"I will never understand how the humans function," Tanahashi said.

"In which way?" Asari asked. "In general, or their society?"

"In any way, really," he replied.

"As I understand it," Geiko, a representative of the oreads, said, "all humans come under the rule of one central power. A king."

"They all follow the same ruler?" Asari asked.

"Yes," she replied. "No matter where the village is

placed, or what family they belong to, they must kneel to one ruler."

"And this king lives here?" Tanahashi asked, pointing to a partially collapsed wall that surrounded a city.

It seemed to be completely constructed from gray stone, molded in some way to create easily stackable building materials. Thatched roofs and wooden details for the windows gave the human capital a dull and monochrome look. Heavy smoke from fires billowed from chimneys and made the area look filthy.

Asari thought he could smell the inhabitants behind the walls. Every fae knew that the humans were dirty creatures, not eager to bathe, leaving their waste wherever they pleased. Their homes were small, but still housed families of up to twelve people. This was done to keep themselves warm, for most of them lived in frigid areas. They often wore thick furs from slain animals to compliment their already hairy bodies.

"The capital is called Ives Grove," Geiko said.

"How come you know so much about the humans?" Aoki asked the oread.

"Oreads deal with humans a lot," she replied. "They come to us with trade, for we are skilled in trapping and agriculture. In return, they supply us with weapons made from steel, which is one of their talents."

"Always preparing for battle," Tanahashi said.

"Not much different from kitsunes," Geiko said with a smile.

"I would not compare us too much to the humans," Asari shot back. "It is a dangerous ground to tread."

"Noted," Geiko replied and winked.

She was right, of course. The kitsunes were born in blood, just like the humans, and the similarities were more than the differences. It was a fact that had always made the kitsunes uneasy.

"Let us head down there before it gets too late," Aoki said. "We can argue about such things once we have the humans on our side."

The others nodded, and they all walked down into the little valley. Ives Grove laid in the center of the seven hills, once constructed to represent the seven original human clans that were united to form their kingdom. Like the faes, the humans had consisted of several clans that waged war against each other until one strong and powerful chieftain forcibly claimed to be the victor.

As they descended the hill, they heard the clamor from the city, which was larger than any of the great cities of the faes, yet most likely not big enough to hold the masses of humans inside. And the smell of it was pungent. It smelled of waste and decay, of death, sickness, and sorrow. On either side of the path they walked, scorched fields spread out, and Asari realized that this city had been attacked by the dragons recently, and that was the reason for the ruined walls and destroyed crops. This might be the reason they needed to convince the humans to join forces.

The gates of the city were open, and a drawbridge was lowered over a dried-up moat. It did little now to keep the attackers out, apart from making them muddy. Dead fish laid in heaps on the bottom, and the horrible stench of death rose from the corpses. Tanahashi covered his mouth with a rag, something he had already sworn to do if they entered the humans' city.

"I feel dirty already," he said in a muffled voice.

"Remember," Asari said back, "we are not here to insult them. So, keep your comments to yourself."

Tanahashi huffed but fell silent.

Strange looks were cast upon them as they crossed under the stone valve that separated the outside world from the city. Winding cobblestone streets swirled in various directions, making strange labyrinthine pathways. Houses were squeezed together so it appeared that new ones had been forcibly built in the dead space between the older ones. It created a second wall inside the first, and some buildings stood several stories high.

Humans, dressed in gray or brown clothes, women with their heads covered in white fabric, sat outside the homes with dirty faces and rotted teeth, and stared at them while their children played. Once in a while, a human would lean out the window and pour a bucket of waste onto the street below. The filth ran down the cobbles and pooled in potholes and other crags.

"If they don't kill us, then disease must surely do so," Aoki said.

"It is one of the fundamental problems with the humans," Geiko said and nodded to an old decrepit man, who was sitting on a rickety stool outside what looked like a meat shop.

The skinned carcasses of rabbits hung in the wide window, while the heads of goats lined the walls of the shop, blood running from them and intermingling with the waste.

"Is that the only thing that separates them from us?" Tanahashi asked.

"The uncleanliness?" Geika replied. "Not really. They are prone to sickness more than us, and they live a shorter life, a mere fifty years at most, just to name a couple."

"So, most of these humans will die soon?" Aoki looked at a child playing in the mud with some wooden figures shaped like warriors.

"To us, yes, but not to them. Their time seems to move much slower than ours. How this works, I do not know."

Asari figured that time didn't actually move slower

for the humans. It had more to do with their lifespan being so short, and they felt rushed all the time. They can fit into a fifty-year lifespan what a fae would accomplish in several hundred.

"How do we find this king?" Asari asked Geiko.

"He usually resides in a castle at the center of the capital," she replied. "We merely continue on this street. All roads lead to the castle."

"Then lead the way," Asari said and held out his hand to her.

They continued to traverse the streets, and as they did, the destruction of the city became more evident. The houses were damaged, large pieces of them missing, the roofs burnt to cinders, and some were nothing more than rubble. They could see the humans, men, women, and children, all hiding under poorly constructed shelters in a desperate attempt to keep nature at bay. Humans had always combated the natural world, while the faes lived as a part of it. They were born from nature and should live in harmony with it, while humans wanted to control and rule it like the king they followed.

It was a sad sight to see, how the mighty humans had fallen and were at the mercy of the elements. In a different lifetime, Asari might have enjoyed the sight, but having experienced it himself, he now pitied them.

There was a steep incline leading to the castle, and

they could see the remains of it atop the little hill that the capital had been built on. It looked like it could have been an impressive structure, a testament to human engineering. Now, it laid in ruins. Towers toppled, walls cracked, and the ground around it scorched.

"There are no troopers around," Geiko said.

"Troopers?" Tanahashi asked.

"It's what the humans call their warriors," she replied. "A special class of humans who work directly under the king."

"Does this mean that they are all dead?" Asari asked.

"Perhaps they perished in a recent dragon attack." Geiko looked around as they approached the ruins.

"What does that mean for us?" Aoki asked.

"The problem is that among the humans, those who are not troopers are all ill-equipped to battle." Geiko sighed.

"So, the humans might not be of any help at all." Asari sounded dejected.

"We shall see."

They walked past the ruined walls that held up no roof, and entered the courtyard that must have been impressive at one point, filled with elaborate decorations and statues. The building stood in juxtaposition to the homes of the regular people. This was made of stone, covered with white marble, but it had mostly collapsed, so the gray rocks were visible.

They then saw a group of humans, dressed in blue tunics that were covered with chainmail, and they each wore a shiny steel skull cap on their head. They were bowing slightly, for in the middle of the courtyard, stood a long wooden table, legs pierced down into the mud that the courtyard had now turned into.

Atop the table laid the body of a man, hands folded over his chest. His eyes were closed, and his long beard was partially scorched, as were his clothes. It looked as if the metal chestplate he wore had slightly melted, wrapped tightly around his body. Like the troopers standing around him, chainmail covered his body, and the ringed hood was pulled over his head.

Geiko cleared her throat to get their attention, and they all turned to the fae standing in their courtyard. Aoki assumed they would go for their weapons, but they never moved a muscle, and he could see the defeat in their eyes.

"We are looking for the king of men," Geiko said in the common tongue.

Everyone in the Far East, no matter the race, spoke the same language. The gods never had a reason to split them up.

"King Eita is dead," a stout man with tears streaming down his face said.

The man was shorter than the other troopers and wore a thin mustache. He was dirty, and his face was covered in ash.

"We are here to offer an alliance against the dragons," Asari said. "Who leads the humans now?"

"I do," the stout man said. It took Asari off guard.

"Who are you?" he asked.

"I am Prince Masato," the man replied. "The king was my father."

"The position of ruler is passed down from parent to child," Geiko explained. "He is now the ruler of all men in the Far East."

"That child?" Tanahashi scoffed. "He doesn't look a day over a hundred."

"I am sixteen," Prince Masato replied.

Tanahashi raised an eyebrow at him, and didn't quite understand how that changed his point.

"We came here to form an alliance with the humans, so that we can defeat the dragons," Asari explained. "But I can see that you have already been defeated. Come, let us leave." He turned to Aoki, Tanahashi, and Geiko. "We have nothing to gain from this. The humans are finished."

They turned around and began to walk away.

"What are you saying?" Masato called out after them. "We are far from being done."

Asari turned around. "What do you have to offer

us?" he shouted back. "A dead leader, a ruined capital, a sad group of warriors, and dejected followers?"

"There is still a will to fight within us." Masato came walking toward them.

"If what we witnessed coming here is any indication of the fighting spirit still within the humans, then I am afraid you can keep it." Asari pointed to the city proper.

"I will have you know, fae." Masato came in close. He was shorter than Asari, but about average for a normal kitsune. The young man stared Asari right in his eyes. "We defended this city on three separate occasions. We fought tooth and nail on those walls before they fell. We lost thousands of men, but several hundred still remain. My father stood with the troopers, shoulder to shoulder, using his sword to kill as many dragons as he could before it became too much. What you see before you is the result of several attacks. You might look at me and see a kid without experience, but I have carried a sword since I was a child. I have waged war against many enemies since that day. If you think there is no fight left in us, think again. This dog can hunt, and I will have retribution for the death of my people, with or without you."

There was a silence between them, the tension thick enough to cut with a knife.

"How many men can you command?" Asari asked.

"As many as you need," Masato said. "I can have my messenger run to the four corners of the Far East and gather all the remaining humans. They can be here within a fortnight."

"Well, then, Prince Masato," Asari smiled, "meet us in Preserve in fifteen days."

ATTACKS FROM THE DRAGONS CONTINUED AS ASARI and his kitsunes scoured the land for survivors. Village after village that they visited produced only a few warriors who were willing to join them. Humans were naturally suspicious of the odd-looking faes at first, similar in appearance but with vastly different parts, but they listened to reason and joined. Blacksmiths and other craftsmen brought their skills and tools to the fight.

"This is the first oni village," Aoki told Asari as they looked down upon the valley. "What do you think?"

"About what?" Asari asked. "If they'd be willing to join us?"

"The onis have always been our enemy," Aoki said. "Wanting to destroy us all throughout history. They might be difficult to convince."

"But they would be great allies," Asari said. "They have crude weapons but are fierce warriors."

"Let's hope for the best." Aoki winked at him.

"WE NEED THE ONIS TO FIGHT ON OUR SIDE," Asari told the oni chieftain.

It was a tiny figure with huge bulging eyes, sharp fangs, and taloned hands. He always had a difficult time telling if they were male or female, or if there was even such a distinction.

"The onis and faes, especially the kitsunes, have been at war since time began," the hunched over figure snarled. "Yet, we understand that there is a need for the children of the universe to stand together."

"We are all in the same boat, chieftain," Aoki said. "This is our army now." He pointed to the group of rag-tag warriors who stood outside the village gates. "We are several hundred strong, and with your help, we might be able to defeat the dragons."

"The onis can do much more than that," the chieftain replied. "We know where the dragons live."

"How is that possible?" Asari asked.

"The onis and dragons once had an alliance," the chieftain explained. "At the dawn of this age, we fought side by side. The Dragon Lord formed an island from melted rock in the South Sea, further away than most faes or humans have traveled. That is where they stay. Where they keep those they kidnap from the battlefields."

"So, you will join us?" Aoki asked.

"We will make a pact with the kitsunes," the chieftain growled. "But only until the dragons are defeated."

SILVIE RETURNED TO THE ISLAND OF DRAGONS after a successful raid on the mainland. She tossed her blade to the side and leaned against the wall. Blood covered every inch of her body, but she didn't care. There was a sensation within her, telling her that she usually did something after coming in from a battle, but she couldn't recall what it was.

Arashi took a seat next to her and placed his head on her shoulder. She kissed his cheek. Like hers, it was stained with patches of crimson from the war. She closed her eyes, happy with what she had accomplished, and the humans she had killed in this raid.

CHAPTER

TWELVE

"It will take us across the sea and drop us off at the island where the dragons live."

The onis all nodded and looked at him. They were not technologically advanced, preferring to fight with their claws and teeth. At times, they would battle with crude, rudimentary weapons made from bamboo or steel, so the concept of traveling on water was new to them.

"The plan is," Asari instructed, "that we surround the island from all directions. In a unified attack so they can't prepare in time."

"The only flaw I can see," a human warrior said, "is how we get there with enough speed to catch them off guard. They must have scouts flying overhead."

"We have a plan for that," the oni chieftain said. "Even if the onis are not used to water, we have strong legs. We shall place onis at the rear of each vessel, and then have them use their legs to move across the sea."

"And we shall add our best archers at the front to hit the damn things in their underbelly," Aoki added.

And thus, the warriors were assembled, a band of unlikely allies standing together as one. Onis, humans, kitsunes, and random faes from all corners of the universe. Together, they would attack the dragons.

They all climbed onto the ships, and the onis placed their lower halves into the water. The kicking of their powerful limbs moved the ships at a high velocity. Asari grabbed the mast to prevent it from falling over as they shot across the surface of the sea.

The onis shifted their kickers from time to time, giving them an opportunity to rest as the boats silently glided toward their destination.

"There it is," the oni chieftain said and pointed

toward the horizon. "The Island of Dragons, a place where no fae or human has ever gone before unless they were prisoners."

Asari was amazed at how easy it was to talk to the oni chieftain. His only encounter with the creatures had either been on the battlefield or as prisoners. And even then, they had only snarled at him and attempted to bite him. No coherent words were spoken at the time.

"It's time to split up!" Asari cried over the waves of water. "We move head on; the rest shall take up position around the island."

Aoki nodded and moved to the aft of the vessel, where he waved a red flag in the air to instruct the other ships. They all split, and the six other ships circled the island. As they did, Asari could see smaller dragon scouts flying along the cliffs. He motioned to Aoki again, who waved another flag, this time, yellow.

The archers at the front of the ships got into position, and at the same time, they all released their arrows. The sky darkened as the hail of wooden projectiles soared through the air. Every single arrow struck, and the dragons collapsed into the sea. The warriors on the boat cheered and continued on.

The call to arms sounded throughout the caves, and dragonmites and dragons alike moved uneasily. Silvie awoken from her dreamless slumber and turned to Arashi, who trembled beside her. She had become used to this call, and was ready to head out to stand with everyone else, but this sound was different. More acute, and she noticed that the dragons appeared more worried than before.

"What is happening?" she asked, but Arashi only growled without giving her an answer.

Silvie rose and headed through the winding hallways and cavernous labyrinth to find her way outside. She was joined by crowds of dragonmites as the dragons alighted and moved toward the sky. Silvie walked over and stood at the edge of the cliff, looking down.

Ships, half a dozen or so, had converged on the island. Dragons rained down from the sky as they were struck in their soft bellies. They howled as they fell.

"This is the last hurrah," a low voice said to her from behind.

She turned around to see Arashi standing there, looking at her with his yellow eyes. In his claw, he held her blade.

"You can talk?" she asked. "I mean, you can still talk?"

"I have always been able to talk," he said and forced a smile. It looked unnatural.

"What do you mean?" Silvie looked confused.

"Dragons and dragonmites can speak without issue," Arashi replied.

"Then why didn't you ever answer me?" Silvie frowned. "I poured my heart out to you, told you my darkest secrets. Fell in love with you and let you in."

"Precisely." Arashi let out something that sounded like a laugh. "If you hadn't, the darkness that permeates this island would not have been able to enter your soul. When the Dragon Lord formed this island from molten rock, he sacrificed part of his own soul."

"I don't understand." Silvie tried to clear her head from the haziness that filled it.

"All who arrive on this island are infected, turned, same with you," Arashi said. "Nothing can change that."

"But the flowers," Silvie whispered and pointed to the red blossoms all around them.

"Those things don't matter; they cannot stop the change."

"But the concoction?"

"Only ordinary liquid to keep our strength up." Arashi looked down at the warriors below, storming the island.

"But everything the aged one spoke of?" Silvie fell to her knees.

"All lies." Arashi turned to her. "All brought about by the darkness inside him. Too weak to fight on our side, so he did what he could. Dragonmites are born this way, no transformation necessary. The true change is done by the humans and faes who turn on their own kind."

Silvie felt something inside her bubbling to the surface. Hatred. Unbridled hatred, but not for the dragons, or for Arashi, whom she had once felt love for. No, it was hatred for her own kind attacking this beloved island. She grabbed the blade and rose.

"Now," Arashi said to her, "let's end them."

ASARI, AOKI, AND THE ONI CHIEFTAIN HAD CHOSEN the cliffside, while the other vessels landed on the beaches or found openings between the island walls to enter through.

"Every kitsune and human, grab onto the back of an oni!" Aoki yelled out to the warriors on the vessel, and they all followed his order.

Asari wrapped his arms around the massive, thick throat of the chieftain.

"You ready?" the chieftain growled.

Asari patted it on the head, and the oni began scaling the wall. He clambered to hold on as the movement of the creature surprised him, and he feared he'd lose his grip. As the chieftain continued to shift its body from left to right, Asari watched the other warriors, holding onto their own onis as they flew up the vertical cliffs, finding their footing at the most impossible of angles.

He looked up to the top edge of the cliff, only to see feathers of fire explode overhead. Smoke and screams were intermingled with the clanging of weaponry and lifeless roars of the dying dragons.

They soon burst over the edge, and both Aoki and Asari climbed off their onis. They looked around to see numerous scorched rocks and bodies of faes, alongside the humans, scattered everywhere.

Several dragonmites came at them, and they took them down with ease. The surprise attack inside the dragons' own home had really caught them off guard, and the warriors seemed to have an advantage. More dragonmites burst from the caves inside the walls, chased by onis and humans troopers, only to be slain by the kitsunes waiting for them at the other end.

"We need to find the heart of the island!" Asari screamed.

"Why?" Aoki replied.

"If we do, then we will find where the greatest

number of dragons are collected," Asari explained. "Killing them will greatly diminish their strength."

"Then let's do so!" Aoki headed for one of the caves, but then he halted.

Standing back-to-back with a dragonmite, he saw his sister, Silvie. She was still dressed in her ragged uniform, and the bamboo armor barely covered her chest. She viciously attacked all the kitsunes, onis, and humans who approached her.

"Silvie!" Aoki screamed, and it caught Asari's attention.

With true purpose, Asari strode toward Silvie, with Aoki in tow. They slashed anyone coming toward them, or allowed others to protect them until the enemy stood eye-to-eye with the two fighters.

Asari stopped in front of Silvie and lowered his sword, staring at the kitsune he loved. She wore a scorn on her face, fierce and filled with hatred. She swung her blade with righteous fury as several onis came toward her.

"Silvie!" Asari called out to her.

"What?" She paused for a moment.

"What are you doing?" Asari asked. "Fighting your own?"

"I am fighting the enemy," she said in a monotonous tone. "Not my own."

"Don't you remember me?" Asari pleaded. "Asari, your love."

"I only have one love," she replied. "And it's not you."

She sprung toward him, blade held high. He parried and stepped back from the impact. She then leaped on him, and they tumbled down the slope together. At the same time, Aoki fought the dragon-mite, Arashi, who used his claws and his maw. Aoki swung back and forth, neither of them gaining ground.

Silvie managed to overpower Asari as they slowly slid toward the edge of the cliff. She looked down at him, the rage of waves breaking down below. He struggled to break free from her grip. He refused to use his blade on her and dropped it to his side instead, focusing on keeping her hands away from him.

"Silvie, don't do this!" he cried as she placed all her weight on him.

Silvie stared intently at him, gritting her teeth as the sharp edge of her weapon closed in on his throat. Then something flashed. It broke through the haze in her mind, like a lighthouse guiding vessels safely to port. Memories of the kitsune under her broke though, visions of them playing together at a cliff's edge. One very much like the one they were on now.

She blinked and shook her head.

"Asari?" she whispered and released her grip.

"Yes, Silvie," he panted. "It is I, Asari."

"I was lied to," she said and sat back, slowly sliding off him. "I was tricked into doing horrible deeds. Killing my own."

"It's okay, Silvie. You're back now." Asari sat up and went to embrace her. "You're back."

But she gently pushed him away and stood up. "I have to end this," she said and spun around.

THIRTEEN

AOKI AND ARASHI PACED AROUND EACH OTHER, breathing heavily and sweating beneath the hot rays of the sun.

"Aoki!" He heard the familiar voice of his sister behind him.

Aoki turned around and saw Silvie running up the slope with a determined look on her face. Arashi took his chance and lunged at him, tearing a gash through his armor and into his tender flesh. Aoki cried out in pain and fell over.

Silvie stepped past him at that moment, unconcerned about her brother's well-being. She lunged at Arashi, who dodged from her body. In her fury, she overreached, and he was atop her. He pressed her into the ground, both his taloned hands on her skull. She could feel a cold sensation emanating from his scaly hands.

"You could have been among the best of us," Arashi whispered to her. "One of our foremost allies, but now, I will erase your mind completely."

He pushed down harder, and she felt the haze of darkness flood her mind, her vision slowly disappearing. She just wanted to give in, tired of struggling against the darkness.

As she took one last breath, the weight left her head. Asari had come over and kicked Arashi in the side, sending him to the ground.

"Are you alright?" he asked her and held out his hand as she turned around.

Before she could answer, the dragonmite had pounced back and clawed him across the face. Silvie tumbled to her feet, blade ready, and plunged her blade directly into the gut of Arashi.

The dragonmite howled as black liquid poured

from his body and flooded the ground, intermingling with the blood of all those who were slain. She pushed it further in, coming close to his body, close like a lover. She kissed him on the check as he tried to breathe through the pain and the realization of imminent death. She then pulled out the blade, and Arashi collapsed onto the ground.

Silvie looked over at Asari, who smiled at her.

"I know these caves," she said. "Let me lead you to victory."

Asari nodded and helped the injured Aoki to his feet. Silvie let out a war cry and ran into a tunnel.

Most of the dragons had long fled, while the dragonmites were stuck to fend for themselves against the onis, kitsunes, and humans. Silvie led her brother and Asari through the labyrinth of tunnels, pointing out at every turn where dragons, dragonmites, or misled prisoners might be hiding. Asari commanded the prisoners to be taken outside so that they could have a chance at being turned away from the darkness as quickly as possible, while warriors slaughtered the rest without mercy.

The team turned several corners as the day passed, until they came upon allies, and then moved down toward another entrance.

Suddenly, the entire island rumbled. It was a quake from the center of the universe. The sea around them rippled with giant ten-foot-tall waves exploding from all directions. Attackers and defenders alike ran from the caves. Some of the dragonmites threw themselves into the water, while most of the faes and onis gathered on the giant grass field in the middle.

The top of the great mountain that stood in the center soon came crashing down as a large dragon broke through the very rock. He stood several feet taller than any other dragon they had seen before. Large scales shook as he twitched his ancient muscles, and enormous spikes protruded from his shoulders and down his back, like the teeth of a large saw. Two wings expanded on either side of him, and as he moved them, the wind pushed several warriors off the island and into the water.

Asari and Silvie stood next to each other, staring at the huge monstrosity that was now before them.

"What in Kami's name is that?" Asari asked in wonder.

"That is the great Dragon Lord," Silvie replied. "The Dragon God."

The Dragon Lord roared at the sky and shook them to the core. Kota came up to Asari and Silvie when he found them, hand clutching his ribs.

"This is our last stand, kitsunes," he said and pointed to the giant dragon. "That beast is the only thing that stands between us and victory. We need to save the Far East now, or we will never have another chance."

"That thing is impossible to defeat!" Asari shouted, shoulders slumped.

"That is typical Eagle and Fox attitude," Kota said and smiled. His mouth was bloody, and his teeth were broken from the battle. "Wolves, join me!" he screamed above the noise that was coming from the Dragon Lord's wings.

A group of no more than ten kitsune warriors rushed over to Kota as he stood there, blade raised in the air.

"Today, we shall not accept defeat!" he screamed. "We give them no mercy! We are so close to victory that we cannot accept failure now."

The Wolves all let out a raucous cheer and raised their weapons.

"After we bring this beast down, I shall personally mount its head onto my wall. A tribute to all who fell today."

Dragon Lord watched the scene unfold below him, as if he were listening to the words of Kota. He smirked and let out a burst of fire from his mouth in defiance.

Kota turned and ran toward the Dragon God, letting out a rallying cry. As they approached the giant claws of the dragon, the Dragon Lord let out one long fiery breath, spewing flames all over the warriors. Several succumbed to the fire, but a few were quick enough to avoid it. They ducked and dodged as the flames scorched the ground where they had just been. Asari, Aoki, and Silvie backed up as far as they could, along with the other assembled fighters.

Kota led the remaining Wolves toward the belly of the Dragon Lord. They climbed the rubble of stone that had been created when the hill toppled from the Dragon Lord breaking through.

With relative ease and quickness, they scaled them. Being so close to the beast, Kota's vision was obscured, and he swung his arms randomly, lashing out as best he could. Large talons dug into the ground, creating large gashes, sending dirt that cascaded in a hail-like pattern.

Some of the Wolves were caught in the rush of air as the claws passed them and sent them flying, their bodies a crushed mess on the rocks before slowly sliding into the sea.

Kota and four other warriors remained, and they jumped from the precipice of the rubble, blades pointing down toward the belly of the Dragon Lord. Every single weapon hit its mark, the steel sinking all the way to the hilt, and the warriors remained dangling. Their legs flapped as the Dragon Lord howled, spewed flames into the air, and twisted and turned.

"There is no way they can hold on!" Aoki shouted. He looked worried.

"They will surely fall to their death if he continues to move!" Silvie yelled back.

"We have to help them!" Aoki gripped his weapon tightly.

"You can't be thinking what I think you are!" Silvie grabbed her brother's shoulder. "It's suicide!"

"If there is one thing I have learned through all of this, sister," Aoki took her hand, "is that you cannot run from your problems. I ran from the Golden Valley to look for something different because I was scared of what might happen if I stayed there. I was scared to come for you when the dragons abducted you. Now I stand here, once again terrified of what may be in my future. But I can't be scared anymore. I have to take hold of my future. The Wolves are right. Take a chance, and never let go."

"But you will die!" Silvie let her tears flow freely.

"Maybe," Aoki removed her hand, "but if that is to be, then I at least died for a reason. I will not sit idly by to die like a true coward."

"You do what you must," Asari came up to them and said.

"Asari!" Silvie pleaded.

"I will not join you," Asari told Aoki. "Someone must stand until the end."

The two Eagles smiled at each other, their arms embraced in a warrior's handshake.

"May Kami protect you," Asari said.

Aoki turned and uttered a roaring cry, equal to that of the Dragon Lord's, and followed the Wolves.

The Dragon Lord was still squirming in a desperate attempt to rid himself of the kitsunes dangling from his underbelly. At the same time, he tried to free his lower body from the island, still trapped.

Kota pulled another blade from a sheath at his side and proceeded to stab the dragon in various places. Black liquid poured from the wounds as the other Wolves did the same. Kota looked over his shoulder and saw an Eagle, Aoki, bouncing up the rubble, blade raised high.

That fool, Kota thought. *In the final throws of battle, he still thinks he can win?*

Suddenly, the Dragon Lord broke free from his island prison. One that he had crafted for himself. The palace where he had plotted at the end of the Far East, where he would claim his victory. It had become a cell of evil, of dark schemes and dreams of vengeance, and no more. Now, he would show the faes and humans exactly what he could do.

The Dragon Lord broke free, his ferocity shaking the ground. As he did so, he fell belly first against the hard surface, crushing everything attached to him. The blades held by the kitsune warriors penetrated his soft flesh, but he only felt the satisfaction of killing the faes who were attached to the metal weapons.

"Aoki!" Silvie screamed as she saw the massive body of the dragon slam into the ground.

"He's fine," Ari said and pointed to Silvie's brother, who was lying on the ground. Luckily, he was further away from the impact when the dragon fell.

"How many men do you have left?" Asari asked the human.

"Can't say," Ari replied. He was covered in black ichor from the slain dragons and dragonmites. "We have been decimated and scattered. We were in the process of expelling the dragonmites in the caves when that thing appeared."

"What do we do now?" Silvie asked. "There is no way we can overpower the Dragon Lord."

"Then we fight until the last fae, human, or oni is gone," Aoki said and stood up.

He had returned, his ego bruised, but unharmed. At that moment, the Dragon Lord rose on all fours. The blood loss and fall seemed to have taken more out of him than he had anticipated, and he looked down at the faes standing before him. Three children of Kami, one child of Kurata, and one hideous creature of Makung. He could kill them all in one fell swoop.

Inside, the Dragon Lord smiled. The thought of punishing the foul gods who had ousted him all those years ago delighted him. He pushed himself up onto his hind quarters and allowed fire to spew from his giant maw. This was going to be good.

Asari, Silvie, Aoki, and Ari had been joined by the oni chieftain. They all stood their ground as the Dragon Lord leaned its head back and shot flames into the air. They all shuddered at the sight of it.

"This is the end, then," Asari said. The others nodded in unison.

"We may have had our differences in the past," Ari lowered his head, "but I have been truly honored to fight alongside the faes and onis on this day."

"Wherever this next life takes us," Silvie said, "I hope we can all reunite again and raise a toast that we all died as heroes."

"Hear, hear!" Aoki pointed his blade at the enormous form of the Dragon Lord. "On this day, all heroes die."

The Dragon Lord came down hard again, his front legs slamming into the ground, causing it to shake.

"All together," Ari commanded to the assembled warriors around them. "Attack!"

Those who were left ran toward the Dragon Lord, who stood ready to fight, when a large crack echoed across the sky. A huge rift split it open, and a bright light shone down on the island. Then it darkened. Like a great shadow had fallen upon them, blocking out the light.

Then the ground below them shook again as a giant man landed on his feet between the warriors and the dragon. The figure, wearing a bronze chestplate and helmet, with sandals and a blue tunic underneath, carried a round bronze shield and a matching sword. He rose and stood at an incredible height, matching the height of the dragon.

"Kurata!" Ari gasped. "He is like all the statues of him."

"Kurata the god?" Silvie asked.

"The very same," Ari replied.

"Dragon Lord," Kurata's voice boomed over them like a thunder clap, "you have gone too far."

"Too far?" The Dragon Lord hissed. "Was this not a competition of what creation could outlive the others?"

"It was," Kurata replied. "But you were not part of this bet."

"Because you and your sisters were afraid of losing." The Dragon Lord smiled.

"No," Kurata retorted. "Because you are not a god, which is evident. Your creations could not defeat the united might of ours. You were forced to come down and meddle in their affairs. That is cheating."

"Cheating or not," the Dragon Lord roared, "I will kill all that you have made, along with you and your sisters. Then, not only will the sky belong to me, but the universe."

"Then you have to get through me!" Kurata raised his shield.

The Dragon Lord attacked with both his front legs. They struck the shield of Kurata, the sound reverberating across the rocks and the sea. Kurata took the full force of the dragon's might, holding onto his balance with his feet planted firmly onto the ground. He swung before the beast could react and managed to cut across the belly, leaving a nasty gash.

The dragon screamed, but then swung its body sideways, clubbing Kurata's legs with its tail. The legs of the god buckled a bit, but he remained upright, raising the shield to meet another blow, this time, from up top. The already weakened legs, with the added weight of the Dragon Lord's massive frame charging at him, pushed Kurata down so that his knees touched the ground. He grunted at the strain of not bending completely.

He tried to swing at his foe, but the Dragon Lord kept him down by pushing harder at the shield, his entire upper body pressed against it. The warriors could see the strain on Kurata's face as he tried to fight against the dragon, but it was becoming too difficult.

"So much for the great warrior god." The Dragon Lord smirked. "In the end, just as easy to crush as his creations."

Kurata managed to find a gap in the scaled feet of the Dragon Lord and slid the point of his sword between his claws. He pushed as hard as he could, and the bronze weapon went deep. The Dragon Lord cried out again and released himself from the shield. Kurata pushed up and sent his shield straight into the snout of the dragon. Once, twice, three times, he smashed it into the maw of the beast. Black blood sprayed from the mouth, and Silvie swore she could see several of the dragon's teeth soar through the air.

The monster fell back against the rubble of stone, and Kurata stood upon him, sword wrenched free and coming down on the thing. The Dragon Lord saw it in time and rolled to the side, but Kurata still caught one of the wings with the blade, tearing it into shreds.

The Dragon Lord tried to fly, but with one wing clipped, it was impossible, his one advantage now gone.

"You should have flown when you had the chance." Kurata spat down at it.

"All the better to stand and fight, then." The Dragon Lord wiped his mouth and charged.

It took Kurata off guard as the hulking mass came at him. They both came down hard onto the ground, leaving a huge crater where their bodies landed. Kurata's sword flew from his grip, and Aoki had to duck to avoid getting hit by it.

Kurata flailed his arms, swinging the shield, but the dragon rained down punches into Kurata's face, denting the bronze helmet in the process. Then he reared up and took a deep breath. The world went silent as the dragon spewed fire in the face of Kurata. White hot flames licked the god's upper torso and head, turning the helmet into liquid bronze, burning the tunic underneath the chestplate completely off. After a full minute, the Dragon Lord gasped for air and stepped back.

Kurata lied there, smoldering, coughing. He wasn't dead yet, but he was hurt. His face was deformed by the blows, and it had turned black from the flames.

"Now you die, god," Dragon Lord scoffed.

"Not today," said a voice from the water.

Suddenly, fourteen other giants rose from the sea. Silvie recognized them as the fae gods, with Kami, the mother of the kitsunes, in the middle. Their hair shone all colors of the rainbow as it moved in the breeze behind them. Dressed in sheer white gowns, they almost glistened in the evening sun. They were beautiful.

"They're all real!" Silvie gasped. "Not tales that we were all foolishly taught to believe."

"You have nothing to gain here." The Dragon Lord

turned to Kami. "I will kill your brother, and then I will do the same to you and your sisters."

"Has the world not suffered enough?" Kami floated through the air. "We created these beings because we wanted to compete with one another. They fought and killed, tried to establish dominance across the universe. A universe that wasn't theirs to dominate. We didn't create the universe for them; we created *them* for the universe. We see the flaws of our creations, but still, we choose to love them. But you, you Dragon Lord, are so filled with spite and hatred that you would sacrifice what you've made in your image just to enact revenge. There has been enough killing."

"Not until I say there's enough!" The dragon hissed.

He reared up again and got ready to breathe out more flames when, all of a sudden, he froze. He winced, and then looked down at his own belly. There, protruding from it, was the tip of a bronze blade. He struggled to keep his eyes open, but they flickered. He fell onto all fours, stumbled slightly, walked over to the edge of the island, then tumbled over the edge and into the sea with a huge splash.

Left standing was Makung, holding the sword of Kurata.

FOURTEEN

THE SEARCH FOR THE REMNANTS OF THE BATTLE continued. Most of the dragons and dragonmites had been defeated, and the humans, faes, and onis moved across the island to find the rest of their enemy.

They trapped them from all sides until every single dragon had been vanquished. As the sun set on the Island of Dragons, the amalgam of warriors gathered on the field, where the red blossoms, now charred remains, had once been.

They cheered in unison, lifting their blades into the air, wet with the black blood of the enemy.

Kami helped the beaten Kurata to his feet and looked down with pride on her and her siblings' creations.

"We can learn much from these creatures," she said to her brother. "Compassion, caring, and acceptance."

"For once, I agree with you, sister." Kurata coughed. "Now take me home so I can heal."

The gods soared into the air and disappeared into the rift in the sky.

The gathered warriors looked after them and smiled. The gods had helped them in their hour of need.

"Let's go home, Asari," Silvie said and placed a hand on his shoulder.

"It has been a long while since we were able to go to a place called home," Asari replied and put his hand on hers.

A HUSH FELL UPON THE LAND AFTER THE LAST battle subsided. The dragons made a vain attempt to attack the mainland, but their decimated army made them easy to fight off.

The information of how to best defend a city from the dragons spread like wildfire. The onis, kitsunes, and humans formed an alliance that traversed the land, city to village to town, in order to stomp out the pockets of remaining dragons. They chased them back across the sea, but also occupied the island so the dragons could not land there and regroup. The onis made their home there instead, so the dragons were forced to fly further away, and hopefully, tire themselves out and crash into the endless sea.

Slowly, the faes, humans, and onis began to rebuild their world, and for the first time, they shared their skills with each other, taking the best from each race. Every village installed a bell in one of their towers, like the one that the Golden Valley had used as their warning system.

The universe slowly returned to normal, but everyone knew that the dragons still might one day return and try to take over the worlds once again.

Silvie decided to remain with Asari and help rebuild Preserve instead of heading back to the Golden Valley with Aoki. The siblings said their goodbyes and parted ways, each creating their own separate future.

"How are you feeling?" Asari asked Silvie as she stood on the scaffolding around the new tower.

She looked down over the cliff, thinking about all the time she'd lost while on the island.

"I'll be fine," she said and turned to look at him, leaning on the railing. "In time, anyway. I can feel the darkness still inside me."

"I'll be by your side to help you through it all." Asari grabbed her hand. "I will always be by your side."

"I know." She smiled and leaned up to kiss him.

She turned around to look out over the cliff again. She wanted to feel happy, but the darkness inside her still clouded her mind.

In time, it shall pass, she thought as she nestled up into Asari's arms.

IN THE REACH OF HEAVEN, THE FAE GODS ONCE again reconvened. Kami looked at her sisters, then at her brothers, Kurata and Makung. For the first time since she could remember, Makung stood proud, his back straight and with what could only be described as a smile on his face. It looked sheepish and awkward, but he did his best.

Next to him, Kurata towered, still broken and bore the scars from the battle. His face was blistered from the fire, and his skin was still healing from the cuts and bruises after being decimated by taloned fists.

"First," he said, turning to his sisters, his voice no longer booming, "I would like to thank you all for using your powers to heal me." His sisters nodded. "Second, I would like to apologize for this entire affair."

"What do you mean?" Kami asked.

"Without my anger, rage, and spite, we wouldn't have had to watch the creations we've built go up in flames. Literally." He tried to smile, but it hurt too much.

"I think we all need to apologize to each other." Kami raised a hand. "We were all vying for a prize that was purely designed to stroke our egos. Self-serving."

"I couldn't agree more." Kaneda spoke next. "We were the ones who didn't care enough about our universe, so we let it destroy itself."

"We have learned a lot over these past years," Khan said. "I, for one, have learned how to love something other than my siblings. I never felt love for the Far East until I created something in my own image, and I will freely admit that I sat up here and watched as they battled for dominance against each other. I smiled at the dastardly deeds they all performed against my fellow faes' creations."

"We have much to be blamed for," Kurata agreed. "We imbued them with our traits, and so they became them. Maybe my creations were the worst of them all."

"Surely, the humans were among the most violent,"

Makung's raspy voice chimed in. "But the onis did unspeakable acts of violence against all the rest without provocation, and for that, I am sorry."

"There is no reason to stand here and take the blame for which creation was worse than the other." Kami stood up. "We all gave our creatures free will, and they did as they pleased to fulfill our plans. It's not fair to vilify them for something we wanted them to do."

"Agreed, sister," Khan said. "We may only regret the demise of some of the faes." She looked down to her feet, and then over to her sisters. "For if you loved them as I loved mine, then I am truly sorry for that loss."

"Let's not dwell upon this," Kami spoke sternly. She was tired of them harping on the same subject every day. "We shall take a page out the book of our creations and work together. They showed us that differences can be settled if a common goal is in sight."

"True, true," her siblings said in unison.

"We shall help them rebuild and repopulate," Kami continued. "Bestow upon them many blessings so that it may ease the transition into a golden age of prosperity."

"Will we show ourselves to them again?" Kaneda asked.

"To some, perhaps," Kami replied. "To those we

find most deserving. Those who could be great leaders in the universe. Those who could help us rebuild. But the important thing is that we shall all be gods to everyone. No longer will it be one god per creation. No, all shall worship freely to whomever they wish, for whatever reason they wish. Let us go out and spread the word to them. Let us show our presence in the beauty of a summer's day, in the spring rain, in the growing of the crops, and in the hopes for new generations born to them. Let us be united for the first time ever."

The gods all raised their glasses and cheered. The booming sound echoed across the Far East, creating a great rumble in the sky.

Silvie's Choice

VIOLA TEMPEST